U0022789

實踐大學 數位出版 合作系列

實用英語文法與基礎段落寫作

Practical English Grammar and Basic Paragraph Writing

實踐大學 曾春鳳

出版心語

　　近年來，全球數位出版蓄勢待發，美國從事數位出版的業者超過百家，亞洲數位出版的新勢力也正在起飛，諸如日本、中國大陸都方興未艾，而臺灣卻被視為數位出版的處女地，有極大的開發拓展空間。植基於此，本組自民國93年9月起，即醞釀規劃以數位出版模式，協助本校專任教師致力於學術出版，以激勵本校研究風氣，提昇教學品質及學術水準。

　　在規劃初期，調查得知秀威資訊科技股份有限公司是採行數位印刷模式並做數位少量隨需出版〔POD＝Print on Demand〕（含編印銷售發行）的科技公司，亦為中華民國政府出版品正式授權的POD數位處理中心，尤其該公司可提供「免費學術出版」形式，相當符合本組推展數位出版的立意。隨即與秀威公司密集接洽，雙方就數位出版服務要點、數位出版申請作業流程、出版發行合約書以及出版合作備忘錄等相關事宜逐一審慎研擬，歷時9個月，至民國94年6月始告順利簽核公布。

　　執行迄今，承蒙本校謝董事長孟雄、陳校長振貴、黃教務長博怡、藍教授秀璋以及秀威公司宋總經理政坤等多位長官給予本組全力的支持與指導，本校諸多教師亦身體力行，主動提供學術專著委由本組協助數位出版，數量近50本，在此一併致上最誠摯的謝意。諸般溫馨滿溢，將是挹注本組持續推展數位出版的最大動力。

　　本出版團隊由葉立誠組長、王雯珊老師、賴怡勳老師三人為組合，以極其有限的人力，充分發揮高效能的團隊精神，合作無間，各司統籌策劃、協商研擬、視覺設計等職掌，在精益求精的前提下，至望弘揚本校實踐大學的校譽，具體落實出版機能。

實踐大學教務處出版組　謹識

2013年1月

Part I

Part I

Practical English Grammar

實用英語文法

Unit 1 Punctuation 標點符號

I Periods / Full Stops (.) 句號

A period is the most commonly used punctuation mark which is used at the end of a declarative sentence.

句號標於句意完整的平述句句尾。

- I am a university student.
- John enjoys reading.
- Mary went to see a movie last night.
- Shih Chien University is located in Taipei.
- Time flies like an arrow.

II Question Marks (?) 問號

A question mark is used at the end of a question.

問號標於問句的句尾。

- What does John enjoy doing?
- Is this book yours?
- What do you usually do in the weekend?
- Why were you late for the meeting this morning?
- Did you miss the school bus this morning?

III Exclamation Marks (!) 感嘆號

An exclamation mark is used at the end of an exclamation. However, it is less common in the academic writing.

感嘆號標於感嘆句的句尾。但是，在正式學術寫作時，極少用此標點符號。

- Watch out!
- Congratulations!
- Surprise!
- Shut up!
- Be quiet!

IV Commas (,) 逗號

ⓐ A comma is used to follow an introductory word or phrase, or an adverb clause before the independent clause.

逗號標於副詞子句或介詞片語與主要子句之間。

- In addition, I am taking some language courses.
  介詞片語　　　　　　　　主要子句
- Since John is a student from the U. S., he has to adapt to this new environment.
  　　　　副詞子句　　　　　　　　　　　主要子句
- If Dave could return to school to finish the high school courses, it would be a
  　　　　　　　　副詞子句　　　　　　　　　　　　主要子句
  tremendous victory.

ⓑ A comma is used to link coordinate (equal) elements in a sentence, and it is also used before the coordinating conjunction in compound sentences.

逗號用於連結句子中詞性或結構相同的字詞，同時逗號也用於複合句的對等連接詞之前。

- Mary loves John, and John loves Mary.　　　（複合句）
- I was so tired last night, so I went home early.　　（複合句）
- Mary likes reading, dancing, and singing.　　（詞性或結構相同的字詞）

ⓒ A comma is used before and after a non-restrictive adjective clause, or a conjunctive adverb that is inserted into the middle of an independent clause.

逗號用於句中插入的非限定用法的形容詞子句前後，或是在句中插入的連接副詞前後。

- My sister, who used to work at a trading company, is an English teacher now.
  　　　　　非限定用法的形容詞子句
- Dr. John Wu, the president of our company, is flying to Taipei tonight.
  　　　　　非限定用法的形容詞子句
- John, however, refused to quit drinking.
  　　　連接副詞

V Semi-colons (;) 分號

A semicolon is used in the following three places:

分號用於下列三個地方：

ⓐ between two sentences which are closely connected in idea

分號標於兩個句意相近或相關的句子之間。

- John loves Mary; Mary loves John.
- He loves the right way; he plays the right ways.
- James loves to play basketball; he usually plays basketball four times a week.

ⓑ before conjunctive adverbs and some transition phrases when they are followed by an independent clause

分號標於連結副詞或轉折詞組之前。（且在連結副詞或轉折詞組之後，要標逗號，再接另一個獨立子句。）

- Drunk driving is dangerous; however, a lot of people still drive after they drink.

ⓒ between items in a series

分號標於一連串項目之間。

- Mary can not decide which hat she likes best: the red hat, with a pink lace; the yellow hat, with a black silk lace; or the white hat, with a green lace.

VI Colons (:) 冒號

Using a colon at the end of an independent clause focuses attention on the words following the colon.

把冒號標於獨立子句之後，可強調跟在冒號後面的字詞。

- There are four people in my family: parents, my younger brother, and I.
- When you come to my office, please bring the following items: pencils, erasers, and markers.

VII Quotation Marks (" ")　引號

Quotation marks are used to enclose direct quotations and unusual words.

引號標於直接引述句子的前後，或有特殊意義的字詞的前後。

ⓐ around direct quotations

引號標於直接引述句子的前後。

- "There is no penalty on bureaus that misuse alternative conscripts. However, regulations to state that servicemen cannot be used in this way," said Dave.
- "There is," said Mr. Huang, "sufficient evidence to think that the parade might endanger national security, social order, or public benefits."

ⓑ around unusual words

引號標於有特殊意義或用意的字詞前後。

- Taiwan's economy can be expected to expand by 2.3 percent this year amid a slowly improving but still "very fragile" global economy.
- The "banquet" consisted of hamburgers, hot dogs, and cola.

VIII Apostrophes (')　撇號

Apostrophes indicate either a contraction or a possession.

撇號可表達兩個字的縮寫，或某個人的所有。

ⓐ contractions（縮寫）

- she's　　　(she is or she has)
- they're　　(they are)
- I've　　　(I have)
- I'd　　　(I would or I had)
- can't　　　(cannot)
- let's　　　(let us)

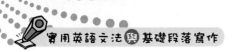

ⓑ possession（所有物）

- John's mother
- the boy's brothers
- children's toys
- my brother's friend
- your father's car

Exercise ❶ 練習一

Add appropriate punctuation in the appropriate places.

請在適當的位置放入適當的標點符號。

❶ Kids love television

❷ In general John enjoys his Japanese and history classes

❸ May said that her husband should send her flowers at least once a week but I told her that was impossible for a man to do so

❹ I am going to Marys house tomorrow night

❺ The test was easy everyone passed it

❻ Dave studies very hard so he usually gets good grades

❼ When I was watching TV a phone rang

❽ A phone rang when I was watching TV

❾ John loves to play basketball he has been playing basketball for five years

❿ Elephants are huge however mice are tiny

⓫ Mice are tiny while elephants are huge

⓬ Mice are tiny on the contrary elephants are huge

⓭ May loves reading she has finished reading at least one hundred books

⓮ Do you smoke

⓯ Look out You almost hit that big rock

1 Kids love television.

2 In general, John enjoys his Japanese and history classes.

3 May said that her husband should send her flowers at least once a week, but I told her that was impossible for a man to do so.

4 I am going to Mary's house tomorrow night.

5 The test was easy; everyone passed it.

6 Dave studies very hard, so he usually gets good grades.

7 When I was watching TV, a phone rang.

8 A phone rang when I was watching TV.

9 John loves to play basketball; he has been playing basketball for five years.

10 Elephants are huge; however, mice are tiny.

11 Mice are tiny, while elephants are huge.

12 Mice are tiny; on the contrary, elephants are huge.

13 May loves reading; she has finished reading at least one hundred books.

14 Do you smoke?

15 Look out! You almost hit that big rock.

Exercise
2　練習二

Add necessary punctuation.

請加上必要的標點符號。

❶ How many people are going to the circus

❷ Six students took the course but only five of them passed the test

❸ The History of Korea which is on the teachers desk is the main textbook for this class

❹ In conclusion doctors are advising people to take more vitamins

❺ George Washington the first president of the United States was a clever military leader

❻ My brother who lives in Taipei has straight brown hair (I have several brothers.)

❼ My brother who lives in Taipei has straight brown hair (I have only one brother.)

❽ When you go to bed make sure you turn off all the lights

❾ Many people have said that it cant be done

❿ The childrens toys were in the living room

練習一

解答

1 How many people are going to the circus?

2 Six students took the course, but only five of them passed the test.

3 The History of Korea, which is on the teacher's desk, is the main textbook for this class.

4 In conclusion, doctors are advising people to take more vitamins.

5 George Washington, the first president of the United States, was a clever military leader.

6 My brother who lives in Taipei has straight brown hair. (I have several brothers.)

7 My brother, who lives in Taipei, has straight brown hair. (I have only one brother.)

8 When you go to bed, make sure you turn off all the lights.

9 Many people have said that it can't be done.

10 The children's toys were in the living room.

Notes

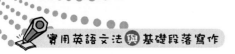

Unit 2 Capitalization 大寫

Basic capitalization rules 基本的大寫原則如下

ⓐ Capitalize the first word of a sentence.

一個句子的第一個字的第一個字母要大寫。

- How many people are going to the circus?
- Taking care of your lawn can be rather simple.
- My sister is a student.
- Dave majors in English.
- Professor Zhang is an excellent teacher.

ⓑ Capitalize proper nouns (including courses offered by organizations or schools).

專有名詞的第一個字母要大寫。

- Dave studies very hard, so he usually gets good grades.
- Mr. and Mrs. Johnson are my neighbors.
- Chiang Kai-Shek Memorial Hall is a famous tourist spot in Taipei.
- The courses I am taking this semester are English Writing, Math, and Economics.
- Dr. Sun Yat-Sen Memorial Hall
- National Palace Museum
- Taipei Fine Arts Museum
- Chinese Lunar New Year

ⓒ Capitalize names of countries, geographic areas, and people from those areas. Capitalize the names of languages and dialects as well.

國名、地理區域、和來自於這些國家及地理區域的人要大寫。各國語言和方言也要大寫。

- My sister, who used to work at a trading company, is an English teacher now.
- Since John is a student from the United States of America, he has to adapt to this new environment.

018

- People from Japan are called Japanese. They speak Japanese.
- I speak Chinese, English, and Taiwanese.

ⓓ Always capitalize the word *I*.

第一人稱 I 要大寫。

- I am from Taiwan.
- There are four people in my family: parents, younger brother, and I.
- The courses I am taking this semester are English Writing, Math, and Economics.
- The lady whom I met last night was Ms. Lee.

ⓔ Capitalize names of months, and days of a week.

月分和星期名稱要大寫。

January	February	March	April	May
June	July	August	September	October
November	December			
Sunday	Monday	Tuesday	Wednesday	Thursday
Friday	Saturday			

ⓕ Capitalize titles of works, books, articles, movies, serials of films, and pieces of art.

作品名稱、書名、文章名稱、電影系列和藝術作品名稱要大寫。

- The Old Man and the Sea
- Sex and the City
- Kinds of Students
- Unchained Melody
- Pride and Prejudice
- Gone with the Wind

Exercise 1 練習一

Add the necessary <u>punctuation</u> and <u>capitalization</u> to the following. Do not change the word order or add or delete any words.

請在下列句子加入必要的標點符號和改為大寫。請勿更動順序或刪減字詞。

❶ John said where is my uniform

❷ Who won the game asked Joan

❸ I can't remember Maggie said where I put my purse

❹ As the students entered the room, the teaching assistant said please take your seats quickly

❺ Jane said I should go to the public library

❻ I asked May are you planning to enter business school

7 My brother June said is a university student

8 My brother is a university student June said he is attending a university

9 My brother is a student he is attending a university she said

10 I'm going to rest for the next two hours Dave said I don't want to be disturbed That's fine I replied you get some rest I'll make sure no one disturbs you

練習一 解答

❶ John said, "Where is my uniform?"

❷ "Who won the game?" asked Joan.

❸ "I can't remember," Maggie said, "where I put my purse."

❹ As the students entered the room, the teaching assistant said, "Please take your seats quickly."

❺ Jane said, "I should go to the public library."

❻ I asked May, "Are you planning to enter business school?"

❼ "My brother," June said, "is a university student."

❽ "My brother is a university student," June said. "He is attending a university."

❾ "My brother is a student. He is attending a university," she said.

❿ "I'm going to rest for the next two hours," Dave said. "I don't want to be disturbed." "That's fine," I replied. "You get some rest. I'll make sure no one disturbs you."

Make necessary corrections.

請將句子改正。

1 wow I cant believe how tall you are

2 does maggie live in west coast apartments too

3 the spring months are february march and april

4 without their ability to use sonar bats would not be able to fly at night

5 ellen and stevens anniversary is may 26 the same day as jerrys birthday

6 there are a lot of mcdonalds fast food restaurants in taipei

7 the intelligent investor written by benjamin graham is considered by many to be one of the most important books ever Written about Investing

8 there are four people in my family they are parents elder brother and i

9 the test was so difficult therefore no one passed it

10 taipei located in the northern part of Taiwan is the capital city of the republic of China

11 i went on a trip to paris this summer

12 dave and mary are getting married this fall

13 dave and mary are getting married this saturday

14 did you have any trouble understanding prof lees lecture today

15 taking multivitamins can be good to my health

16 i like to call my friends because I want to hear my friends voices

17 do you prefer to call or text your friends when you need to tell them something

18 it was really scary when i saw a tall thin man with a shiny silver gun in his hand coming toward me

19 how quickly can a student write in english

20 in fact it is good for students to speak more than one language

① Wow! I can't believe how tall you are.

② Does Maggie live in West Coast Apartments too?

③ The spring months are February, March, and April.

④ Without their ability to use sonar, bats would not be able to fly at night.

⑤ Ellen and Steven's anniversary is May 26, the same day as Jerry's birthday.

⑥ There are a lot of McDonald's Fast Food Restaurants in Taipei.

⑦ The Intelligent Investor, written by Benjamin Graham, is considered by many to be one of the most important books ever written about investing.

⑧ There are four people in my family; they are parents, elder brother, and I.

⑨ The test was so difficult; therefore, no one passed it.

⑩ Taipei, located in the northern part of Taiwan, is the capital city of the Republic of China.

⑪ I went on a trip to Paris this summer.

⑫ Dave and Mary are getting married this fall.

⑬ Dave and Mary are getting married this Saturday.

⑭ Did you have any trouble understanding Prof. Lee's lecture today?

⑮ Taking multivitamins can be good to my health.

⑯ I like to call my friends because I want to hear my friends' voices.

⑰ Do you prefer to call or text your friends when you need to tell them something?

⑱ It was really scary when I saw a tall thin man with a shiny silver gun in his hand coming toward me.

⑲ How quickly can a student write in English?

⑳ In fact, it is good for students to speak more than one language.

Notes

Unit 3 Sentence Structures 句型

A sentence is a group of words that contains at least one subject and one verb. A sentence expresses a complete thought and is formed from one or more clauses. There are four kinds of sentences in English: *simple* sentences, *compound* sentences, *complex* sentences, and *compound-complex* sentences.

一個句子是一群字的組合，其中至少包含一個主詞和一個動詞。一個句子表達一個完整的意念，由一個或多個子句組成。

英語句型分為四類：簡單句、複合句、複雜句、和複合複雜句。

I Simple Sentences 簡單句

A simple sentence has one subject and one verb, and is one independent clause. If the verb in a simple sentence is a transitive verb, it is necessary to put a complement after the verb. If the verb in a simple sentence is an intransitive verb, it is not necessary to have a complement after the verb.

一個簡單句中，有一個主詞和一個動詞，並且是一個獨立子句。如果簡單句中的動詞是一個及物動詞，則動詞之後要加一個補語，當成是及物動詞的受詞。如果簡單句中的動詞是一個不及物動詞，則不需要加補語。

	Subject（主詞）	+ Verb（動詞）	+ Complement（補語）
及物動詞	I	like	music.（名詞）
	Children	love	toys.（名詞）
	I	couldn't recognize	you.（代名詞）
	My son	owns	his own store.（名詞片語）
	David	wants	to get married.（動詞片語）
不及物動詞	Both Tim and Ted	work.	
	My head	hurts.	
	John	studies and works.	
	Birds	fly.	

※但是，不及物動詞後面，可加介詞片語或是副詞，來完整句子的意義。

Birds	fly	in the sky.（介詞片語）
It	is raining	now.（副詞）

II Compound Sentences　複合句

A compound sentence is composed of two simple sentences (two independent clauses) which are connected by a comma and a coordinating conjunction. There are seven coordinating conjunctions in English: **and, but, so, or, for, nor,** and **yet**. Use a comma before the coordinating conjunction in compound sentences.

複合句是兩個簡單句（獨立子句）的組合。兩者之間要加一個對等連接詞（**and，but，so，or，for，nor，yet**），且在對等連接詞之前，要加一個逗點。

- Emma is a good student, and she always gets good grades.
- My elder brother is strong, but my younger brother is weak.
- Alice is very kind, so everyone likes her very much.
- I have to get up early tomorrow morning, or I will miss my class.
- Mary stayed up late last night, for she had to finish her project.
- There is no water in the desert, nor is there any tree.
- Jane is a funny girl, yet you can't help liking her.

A second way to form a compound sentence is add a conjunctive adverb to connect two simple sentences. Remember to put a semicolon before and a comma after the conjunctive adverb.

第二種複合句的組成方法是在兩個簡單句之間，加入一個連接副詞去連接兩個簡單句。記得在連接副詞之前要加一個分號，連接副詞之後要加一個逗號。

- Schools offer preparation for many occupations; besides/moreover/in addition, they prepare students to go for advanced research.
- I have to take final examinations; otherwise, I will receive a grade of Incomplete.
- The cost of living in big cities is high; however/nevertheless/still, the population of big cities is usually rising.

A third way to form a compound sentence is to connect two simple sentences with a semicolon. Remember this is possible only when the two simple sentences are closely related in meaning.

第三種複合句的組成方法是用一個分號去連接兩個簡單句。這種方法只用在連接的這兩個簡單句在意義上相近。

> ● Two hundred guests attended Mary's birthday party; three hundred guests attended her wedding banquet.

III Complex Sentences 複雜句

A complex sentence contains one independent clause and one (or more) dependent clause(s). Here, dependent clauses include adverb, adjective, and noun clauses.

一個複雜句包含一個獨立子句和一個或多於一個的附屬（非獨立）子句。在此，附屬（非獨立）子句包括副詞子句、形容詞子句、名詞子句。

ⓐ complex sentences with adverb clauses 帶副詞子句的複雜句

▶ 1 to tell why: 表原因

because, since, as, now that

> ● **Because** he stayed up late last night, he didn't come to school.
> ● Tom decided not to go to the party **since** he didn't know anyone there.
> ● Mary decided to go to a movie **as** she didn't have anything to do.
> ● **Now that** John has a new car, he could drive to his office.

▶ 2 to show time relationships: 表時間

when, while, as, until, after, before, by the time, whenever, as soon as, as long as, so long as

> ● **When** my mother came home this afternoon, I was talking on the phone.
> ● **While/As** I was walking home, my phone rang.
> ● They will stay there **until** they finish their project.
> ● Mary will go abroad **after** she graduates.
> ● **Before** Tom came this morning, Jane (had) left.
> ● **By the time** David arrives next week, we will already have left.
> ● **Whenever** I see my teacher, I smile and say hello.

* Marie will leave for Taipei **as soon as** it stops raining.
* **As long as** I live, I will never speak to David.

▶ **3** to show opposition:　表矛盾對比

　　(even) though, although, while, whereas

* **(Even though)/Although** it rained, Tom went to school.
* John is tall, while/whereas Tim is short.
* Whereas/While Tim is short, John is tall.

▶ **4** to express conditions:　表條件

　　(even) if, whether (or not), unless

* (Even) **if** it is cold tomorrow, I will stay home.
* I will stay home whether (**or not**) it is cold tomorrow.
* I will go swimming tomorrow **unless** it is very cold.

ⓑ complex sentences with adjective clauses　帶形容詞子句的複雜句

* She is the woman **whom** I saw last night.
* Anyone **who** wants to go with me is welcome.
* The courses **that/which** I am taking this semester are interesting.
* Taipei, (**which is**) the capital city of the Republic of China, is located in the northern part of Taiwan.
* We really liked the small town **where** we spent our vacation this year.
* A woman **whose** purse was stolen called the police.
* There is the man **whose** picture was in the newspaper.

ⓒ complex sentences with noun clauses　帶名詞子句的複雜句

question words: **(when, who, what, why, which, how), whether (or not), that**

* I don't know **when** he arrived.
* I don't know **who** she is.
* **What** he said was not true.
* **Why** he left the country was a secret.
* Do you know **which** color he likes?

- Do you know **how** old a person has to be to get a driver's license?
- I wonder **whether** she will come (**or not**).
- **Whether** Jane comes (**or not**) is important to Tom.
- **That** Jane doesn't love David is obvious.

Ⅳ Compound-Complex Sentences 複合複雜句

A compound-complex sentence has at least three clauses, at least two of which are independent.

一個複合複雜句中至少包含三個子句，且在三個子句之中，至少有兩個子句是獨立子句。

- I like romance movies, **but** my brother likes science fiction movies **because** science fiction movies have excellent special effects.
- **After** I graduated from university, I planned to go abroad to study, **but** I had to work to support my family.
- John had to finish his homework **before** he went to bed, **or** he would be punished by the teacher on the following day.
- Drunk driving is dangerous; **however**, a lot of people still drive **after** they drink.
- May told her husband **that** he should send her flowers on her birthday this year; **nevertheless**, he still forgot to do so.
- Two hundred guests attended Mary's birthday party **which** was held in the Grand Hotel; three hundred guests attended her wedding banquet **which** was held in Taipei 101.

An independent clause is a complete sentence, but a dependent clause is an incomplete sentence. Write Indep. next to the complete sentences, capitalize the first letter at the beginning of the sentences and put a period (.) at the end of the sentences.

一個獨立子句就是一個完整的句子，但是，一個非獨立子句只是一個不完整的句子而已。請先辨認出完整的句子，將句子的第一個字母大寫，句尾加上句點，並在句子前寫下 *Indep.* 表示是一個完整的句子。

_____ ❶ Mary failed in the math test

_____ ❷ because she didn't study hard

_____ ❸ when you go to a movie next time

_____ ❹ he is the man whom I love

_____ ❺ a shirt that has three buttons missing

_____ ❻ that the world is round

_____ ❼ why you lie to me

_____ ❽ scientists do not know what kind of virus causes the illness

_____ ❾ whether you like it or not

_____ ❿ please tell me where the student dorm is

_____ ⓫ for a delicious but inexpensive meal

_____ ⓬ choosing the right classes can be stressful

_____ ⓭ cut the cake into ten pieces

_____ ⓮ my brother who is a doctor

_____ ⓯ young people enjoy Harry Porter serials

_____ ⓰ now that you are a big boy

_____ ⓱ May enjoys reading

_____ ⓲ while Tim was on his way to school

_____ ⓳ maybe if I am good

_____ ⓴ thousands of puppies are bought every day in Taiwan

練習一 解答

Independent clauses:

❶ Mary failed in the math test.

❹ He is the man whom I love.

❽ Scientists do not know what kind of virus causes the illness.

❿ Please tell me where the student dorm is.

⓬ Choosing the right classes can be stressful.

⓭ Cut the cake into ten pieces.

⓯ Young people enjoy Harry Porter serials.

⓱ May enjoys reading.

⓴ Thousands of puppies are bought every day in Taiwan.

Exercise 2 練習二

Identify the subjects, verbs, and complements in the following sentences.

請辨認出句子的主詞、動詞、補語。

❶ There are five students in the classroom.

❷ My name is Mike Rogers.

❸ In Taiwan, there are a lot of beautiful temples.

❹ Joe was born on January 1, 1998, in Taipei, Taiwan, R.O.C.

❺ Do you have any solution to this problem?

❻ Three buttons were missing.

❼ Dr. Chang is the chairman of this department.

❽ My brother and sister are students.

❾ Lungshan Temple is a famous tourist spot in Taiwan.

❿ Would you like to have a cup of coffee?

⓫ Did you use to collect stamps?

⓬ He came and began to talk on the phone with his friend.

⓭ How often do you go to the movies?

⓮ How many hours of sleep do you get every night?

⓯ Tell me your pastimes.

❶ There <u>are</u> <u>five students</u> in the classroom.
    S. V.   C.

❷ <u>My name</u> <u>is</u> <u>Mike Rogers</u>.
    S.   V.   C.

❸ In Taiwan, <u>there</u> <u>are</u> <u>a lot of beautiful temples</u>.
   C.   S. V.   C.

❹ <u>Joe</u> <u>was born</u> <u>on January 1, 1998, in Taipei, Taiwan, R.O.C.</u>
  S.   V.   C.

❺ Do <u>you</u> <u>have</u> <u>any solution to this problem</u>?
     S. V.   C.

❻ <u>Three buttons</u> <u>were missing</u>.
      S.   V.

❼ <u>Dr. Chang</u> <u>is</u> <u>the chairman of this department</u>.
    S.   V.   C.

❽ <u>My brother and sister</u> <u>are</u> <u>students</u>.
        S.   V. C.

❾ <u>Lungshan Temple</u> <u>is</u> <u>a famous tourist spot in Taiwan</u>.
      S.   V.   C.

❿ Would <u>you</u> <u>like</u> <u>to have a cup of coffee</u>?
      S. V.   C.

⓫ Did <u>you</u> <u>use to</u> <u>collect stamps</u>?
     S. V.   C.

⓬ <u>He</u> <u>came and began</u> <u>to talk on the phone with his friend</u>.
  S.   V.   C.

⓭ How often do <u>you</u> <u>go</u> <u>to the movies</u>?
          S. V.   C.

⓮ How many hours of sleep do <u>you</u> <u>get</u> <u>every night</u>?
      C.   S. V.   C.

⓯ <u>Tell</u> <u>me</u> <u>your pastimes</u>. （命令句中，主詞you省略。）
  V.   C.

Identify the following sentences. Write Simple, Compound, Complex, or Compound-Complex next to them.

請辨認以下句子為簡單句、複合句、複雜句或是複合複雜句。

_____ ❶ Could you tell me where the post office is?

_____ ❷ He lives in a small town which is near Tainan.

_____ ❸ John loves Mary, but Mary loves David.

_____ ❹ If it rains tomorrow, we will stay at home.

_____ ❺ I think I met that man at Bob's party last week.

_____ ❻ Some people think that they have a right to buy puppies, but they have a responsibility to take care of them as well.

_____ ❼ If I were you, I would tell him the truth.

_____ ❽ He was sick, yet he went to school.

_____ ❾ As soon as he arrived at home, he received a call from his father.

_____ ❿ When Jim is working, nothing can distract him or slow him down.

_____ ⓫ My cousin is turning five next week, and I am going to buy a gift for him.

_____ ⓬ Hurry up, or you would miss your bus.

_____ ⓭ We went to some KTVs last night.

_____ ⓮ One day, we went to a park and saw some young kids.

_____ ⓯ One day, we went to a park and saw some young kids who were in strange suits.

_____ ⓰ One day, we went to a park and saw some young kids who were in strange suits, and they told us some interesting stories.

_____ ⓱ Every morning, I get up, have my breakfast, and catch my school bus.

_____ ⓲ Next time I meet James, I would return him his notebooks.

_____ ⓳ I am going to take the driving lesson now that I am twenty.

_____ ⓴ Before I came to work, I called my brother, but he wasn't home.

練習三　解答

Simple sentences: 13, 14, & 17

Compound sentences: 3, 8, 11, & 12

Complex sentences: 1, 2, 4, 5, 7, 9, 10, 15, 18, & 19

Compound-Complex sentences: 6, 16, & 20

Notes

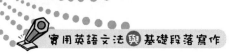

Unit 4 Noun Clauses 名詞子句

A noun clause is used as **a subject** or **an object**.
名詞子句的性質如同一個**主詞**或**受詞**；也就是說，名詞子句可當一個主詞或受詞來用。

I Words used to introduce noun clauses 引導名詞子句的字詞

a question words:

when	where	why	how	who	whom
what	which	whose	-ever words (whoever, whatever, wherever,..)		

- I don't know <u>where Mary lives</u>.
  當成know的受詞
- I could hear <u>what Tom said</u>.
  當成hear的受詞
- Do you know <u>who lives there</u>?
  當成know的受詞
- I wonder <u>whose pen that is</u>.
  當成wonder的受詞
- Do you know <u>why Mary dropped out of school</u>?
  當成know的受詞
- I can't remember <u>how much this watch costs</u>.
  當成remember的受詞
- <u>What we are doing in this class</u> is easy.
  當成本句的主詞
- <u>What Tom said</u> wasn't true.
  當成本句的主詞
- <u>Who is the mayor of this city</u> is not important.
  當成本句的主詞
- <u>How long a butterfly lives</u> is amazing.
  當成本句的主詞
- You can talk to <u>whomever you choose</u>.
  當成介詞to的受詞
- The doctor gave allergy medicine to <u>whomever wanted it</u>.
  當成介詞to的受詞

ⓑ whether/if

- ⓖ I don't know whether (or not) Mary will come.
- ⓖ I don't know whether Mary will come or not.
- ⓖ I wonder whether Mary needs help.
- ⓖ I don't know if May will come (or not).
- ⓖ Whether May needs help is not important at all.

ⓒ that

- ⓖ I think that John is a good student.
- ⓖ I think John is a good student. (Frequently that is omitted in speaking.)
- ⓖ Everyone knows that the world is round.
- ⓖ That John is a good student is true.
- ⓖ That the world is round is a fact.
- ⓖ It is true that John is a good student.
- ⓖ It is a fact that the world is round.

⭑ A"that clause" is frequently used with *the fact*.

- ⓖ The fact that Ann was late didn't surprise me.
- ⓖ The fact that Dave is frequently absent from class indicates his lack of interest in school.
- ⓖ I feel fine except for the fact that I'm a little tired.
- ⓖ Jane was not admitted to the university due to the fact that she didn't pass the entrance examination.

Exercise 1 練習一

Identify Noun Clauses. Underline the noun clauses.

請辨認名詞子句，並在子句下畫線。

❶ Many people believe that the ghosts in the underworld would come out in the seventh month of the Chinese Lunar Calendar.

❷ The fact that the world is round is true.

❸ Children were amazed by the stories that Mary told them.

❹ Children were amazed by what Mary told them.

❺ What he has done to my sister was not forgivable.

❻ Mrs. Wang gave David what he deserved.

❼ I would apply what I have learned to my work.

❽ Is it true that John and Mary are getting married?

❾ I was wondering why you could not finish your assignment on time.

❿ Can you tell me which way the post office is?

❶ Many people believe <u>that the ghosts in the underworld would come out in the seventh month of the Chinese Lunar Calendar</u>.

❷ <u>The fact that the world is round</u> is true.

❸ Children were amazed by the stories that Mary told them. (no noun clauses)

❹ Children were amazed by <u>what Mary told them</u>.

❺ <u>What he has done to my sister</u> was not forgivable.

❻ Mrs. Wang gave David <u>what he deserved</u>.

❼ I would apply <u>what I have learned</u> to my work.

❽ Is it true <u>that John and Mary are getting married</u>?

❾ I was wondering <u>why you could not finish your assignment on time</u>.

❿ Can you tell me <u>which way the post office is</u>?

Complete Noun Clauses.
請完成下列的名詞子句。

❶ (What kind of part time jobs do you have?)

I was wondering _____

❷ (How often do you go to the movies?)

Can you tell me _____

❸ (Did you like your job?)

I was wondering _____

❹ (What is your greatest strength?)

Can you tell me _____

❺ (Why are you changing jobs?)

Could you explain _____

❶ I was wondering <u>what kind of part time jobs you had</u>.

❷ Can you tell me <u>how often you go to the movies</u>?

❸ I was wondering <u>whether you liked your job or not</u>.

❹ Can you tell me <u>what your greatest strength is</u>?

❺ Could you explain <u>why you are changing jobs</u>?

Imagine you are witnesses at the scene of a traffic accident. A pedestrian was hit by a truck, but the driver hit and ran. Take turns asking and answering the police officer's questions. Use a wh-clause and a statement of uncertainty: I don't remember, I'm not sure, or I don't know.
想像你現在是一起車禍的目擊證人：有位行人被一輛卡車撞到，但駕駛肇事逃逸。輪流提問和回答警察的問題，回答請用wh-子句表其不確定性，如：我不記得……、我不確定……、我不知道……。

例：Where is the victim?
I'm not sure where he/she was.

❶ Was he/she hurt?

❷ How old is he/she?

❸ What time did the accident occur?

❹ What did the truck look like?

❺ What color was the truck?

❻ Who was driving the truck?

❼ What did the driver look like?

❽ How fast was the truck going?

❾ What was the license plate number on the truck?

❶ I'm not sure if he/she was hurt.

❷ I don't know how old he/she was.

❸ I'm not sure when the accident occurred.

❹ I don't remember what the truck looked like.

❺ I don't remember what color the truck was.

❻ I'm not sure who was driving the truck.

❼ I'm not sure what the driver looked like.

❽ I'm not sure how fast the truck was going.

❾ I don't remember what the license plate number on the truck was.

II Quoted Speech (Direct Speech) vs. Reported Speech (Indirect Speech) 直述引語和轉述引語

Quoted Speech (Direct Speech)	Reported Speech (Indirect Speech)
"The book is on my desk."	May *says* **that the book is on her desk**.
"Are you leaving?"	Tim *asked (me)* **if I was leaving**.
"Do you watch TV?"	Joe *asked (me)* **if I watched TV**.
"Where did you go?"	I *asked* **where Tim had gone**.
"Press the red button."	Mary *told* Tim to **press the red button**.
"Don't press the red button."	Mary *said* **not to press the red button**.
"It's raining."	Joe *says* **that it's raining**.
"It rained."	Joe *says* **that it rained**.
"It's going to rain."	Joe *says* **that it's going to rain**.
"I'm working."	Tim *said* **that he was working**.
"I left early."	Tim *said* **that he had left early**.
"I've finished my homework."	Bob *said* **that he had finished his homework**.
"I will see you later."	Bob *said* **that he would see me later**.
"I'm going to win."	Tim *said* **that he was going to win**.
"You may watch TV."	Tim *said* **that I might watch TV**.
"I have to try."	Tim *said* **that he had to try**.
"I must take a vacation."	Tim *said* **that he had to take a vacation**.
"You should work harder."	May *said* **that I should work harder**.
"You ought to stay here."	May *said* **that I ought to stay there**.

ⓐ Talking about What People Have Said - Reported Speech 轉述引語

When speakers want to talk about what others have said, they can use either quoted speech, in which the words are repeated exactly, or they can use reported speech.

Quoted Speech 直述引語	Reported Speech 轉述引語
"I won't be late."	Bob said that he wouldn't be late.

When reported speech is used, certain grammatical changes must be made in the words that someone has said.

要將**直述引語**改為**轉述引語**時，句子中的動詞時態要改變。

▶**1** Statements　敘述

(a) Verbs in the present tense change to the past tense.
現在式動詞改為過去式動詞。

> ☞ "I really **like** mystery stories."
> ☞ He said that he really **liked** mystery stories.

(b) Verbs in the present perfect change to the past perfect.
現在完成式動詞改為過去完成式動詞。

> ☞ "I **haven't been** to a party in ages."
> ☞ She said that she **hadn't been** to a party in ages.

(c) *Will* changes to *would, can* to *could*, and *may* to *might*.
will，can，may助動詞的時態，由現在式改為過去式。

> ☞ "I **will help** you with your homework."
> ☞ He said he **would help** me with my homework.
> ☞ "I **may call** you tonight."
> ☞ She said that she **might call** me tonight.
> ☞ "He **can't understand** the lesson."
> ☞ She said that he **couldn't understand** the lesson.

(d) In theory, the past tense changes to the past perfect, but it is often left unchanged, especially in spoken English.
動詞的時態由過去式改為過去完成式，但在口說時，通常保持過去式。

> ☞ "I **didn't go** to sleep until 3:00 a.m."
> ☞ She said she **hadn't gone** to sleep until 3:00 a.m.
> ☞ She said that she **didn't go** to sleep until 3:00 a.m.　（口說時，保持過去式。）

After **say**, the more frequent reporting verb is **tell**. **Tell** differs from **say** in that it is always followed by an indirect object.

直述引語的動詞為**say**時，改為**轉述引語**時，動詞改為**tell**，且必須加一個間接受詞來當成**tell**的受詞。

● David said, "I won't be late."

➡ David told **me** that he wouldn't be late.

      間接受詞

● Mary said, "I haven't been to a party in ages."

➡ Mary told **me** that she had'nt been to a party in ages.

      間接受詞

***That** is often omitted after the reporting verb, especially in conversation.

▶**2** Questions　問句

(a) The word order in wh- questions is the same as for statements, and *do, does*, and *did* are not used.

● "Where does Norma live?"   He asked me where Norma lived.

● "What did Jack say?"   She asked me what Jack said.

(b) With yes/no questions, *if* or **whether** must be used.

● "Can you help me?"   She asked **if** I could help her.

● "Are you going home?"   He asked **whether** I was going home.

▶**3** Commands　命令

Commands use the words **tell, order**, or **command** as the verb, and add an object (the person spoken to) and an infinitive (the command the person spoken to should do) after the verb.

直述引語若是命令句，改為**轉述引語**時，動詞改為**tell**，**order**，或**command**，且動詞後面必須加一個受詞（受命令者），受詞後面再接一個不定詞片語（受命令者必須做的事）。

● "Give me all the keys."　命令句（肯定）

   Susan **told**   **me**   **to give** her all the keys.

        受詞   不定詞片語

◐ "Don't forget your hat." 命令句（否定）

    Susan **told**   <u>**him**</u>   <u>**not to forget** his hat</u>.

                     受詞   不定詞片語

Exercise 4 練習四

Change the following sentences into reported speech.
請將下列句子改為轉述引語。

1 "I can't type," I told them.

2 "Are you English?" they asked me.

3 "Where are you going?" I asked her.

4 "My parents had gone to bed," she said.

5 "We're going into town," they said.

6 "You should go to the doctor," she told him.

7 "I haven't got any money," he told me.

8 "We'll do the dishes," they promised.

9 "Can you phone the doctor for me?" she asked him.

10 "I don't know what to do," I said.

11 "My headache was getting worse, so I went to the doctor yesterday," Jack said.

12 "Can you lend me some money?" he asked me.

13 "What time did you get home?" they asked him.

14 "I passed my driving test last Friday," he told his boss.

15 "Don't be stupid," she told me.

16 "Did you enjoy the film?" I asked her.

17 "Would you wait outside for a few minutes?" he asked me.

18 "Don't forget your hat," she reminded him.

19 "Don't touch the wire," he warned me.

20 He asked, "Are you married or single?"

❶ I told them that I couldn't type.

❷ They asked me if I was English.

❸ I asked her where she was going.

❹ She told me that her parents had gone to bed.

❺ They told me that they were going into town.

❻ She told him that he should go to the doctor.

❼ He told me that he hadn't got any money.

❽ They promised that they would do the dishes.

❾ She asked him whether he could phone the doctor for her.

❿ I told him that I didn't know what to do.

⓫ Jack told me that his headache had been getting worse, so he had gone to the doctor the day before.

⓬ He asked me if I could lend him some money.

⓭ They asked him what time he had got home.

⓮ He told his boss that he had passed his driving test on the previous Friday.

⓯ She told me not to be stupid.

⓰ I asked her if she had enjoyed the film.

⓱ He asked me if I would wait outside for a few minutes.

⓲ She reminded him not to forget his hat.

⓳ He warned me not to touch the wire.

⓴ He asked me if I was married or single.

Exercise 5 練習五

Make your own complex sentences (with a noun clause) with the following phrases.
請用下列句型造出帶有名詞子句的複雜句。

❶ My mother promised…

❷ I offered…

❸ The doctor advised my brother…

❹ Bob wanted to know…

❺ I don't remember…

❻ I wondered…

❼ Could you tell me…

❽ It is true…

❾ _____ made Tom angry.

❿ Do you know…

練習五 解答

Answers will vary.

For example:

❶ My mother promised me that I could have my own room.

❷ I offered him that I could help him with his homework.

❸ The doctor advised my brother that he should take a rest.

❹ Bob wanted to know if he passed the test (or not).

❺ I don't remember if I locked the door.

❻ I wondered what he was going to do next.

❼ Could you tell me where the post office is?

❽ It is true that Ms. Lee has got a promotion.

❾ What Mary said made Tom angry.

❿ Do you know why John dropped out of school?

Exercise 6 練習六

Add the necessary punctuation and capitalization to the following.
請在下列句子加入必要的標點符號和改為大寫。

❶ Larry said mary there is a phone call for you

❷ mary there is a phone call for you larry said

❸ mary there is said larry a phone call for you

❹ There is a phone call for you it's your sister said larry

❺ There is a phone call for you he said it's your sister

❻ I asked him where is the phone

❼ where is the phone she asked

❽ i think said mary i am going to buy a new skirt to go with my shoes

❾ do you want to go with me tom asked if you have time

❿ do you know where tom lives may asked

⓫ if it is possible would you prefer to go the concert with david may asked

⓬ jerry said it is difficult to find a parking space in taipei

❶ Larry said, "Mary, there is a phone call for you."

❷ "Mary, there is a phone call for you," Larry said.

❸ "Mary, there is," said Larry, "a phone call for you."

❹ "There is a phone call for you. It's your sister," said Larry.

❺ "There is a phone call for you," he said. "It's your sister."

❻ I asked him, "Where is the phone?"

❼ "Where is the phone?" she asked.

❽ "I think," said Mary, "I am going to buy a new skirt to go with my shoes."

❾ "Do you want to go with me," Tom asked, "if you have time?"

❿ "Do you know where Tom lives?" May asked.

⓫ "If it is possible, would you prefer to go the concert with David?" May asked.

⓬ Jerry said, "It is difficult to find a parking space in Taipei."

Complete the sentences by changing quoted speech to reported speech.
請將直述引語改為轉述引語，並完成句子。

❶ Andy asked me, "What time does the movie begin?"

Andy wants to know _____

❷ Fred asked, "Can we still get tickets for the concert?"

Fred asked _____

❸ Jim said, "I have finished my work."

Jim said that _____

❹ Tom said, "Don't move."

Tom told me _____

❺ David said, "When did you arrive?"

David asked me that _____

❻ John said, "Are you comfortable?"

John asked me _____

❼ "What time does the train leave?" I asked.

I don't know _____

❽ "Show me your driver's license," said the police officer.

The police officer asked me _____

❾ "Why did they leave the country?"

_____ is a secret.

❿ "My headache was getting worse, so I went to the doctor yesterday,"

Jack said. _____

❶ Andy wants to know <u>what time the movie begins</u>.

❷ Fred asked <u>if they could still get tickets for the concert</u>.

❸ Jim said that <u>he had finished his work</u>.

❹ Tom told me <u>not to move</u>.

❺ David asked me that <u>when I had arrived</u>.

❻ John asked me <u>if I was comfortable</u>.

❼ I don't know <u>what time the train leaves</u>.

❽ The police officer asked me <u>to show him my driver's license</u>.

❾ <u>Why they left the country</u> is a secret.

❿ Jack said <u>that his headache had been getting worse, so he had gone to the doctor the day before</u>.

Unit 5) Adjective Clauses / Relative Clauses 形容詞子句

1. Relative clauses can be thought of a combination of two sentences. They are dependent clauses and they must be attached to a main clause. Therefore, relative classes have a subject and verb and follow the noun they refer to.

   附屬子句可視為兩個句子的組合。他們是非獨立子句,他們必須附屬於一個主要子句之下。因此,附屬子句中有一個主詞和一個動詞,且這個附屬子句必須緊跟在它所修飾的名詞後面。

2. An adjective clause uses pronouns to connect the dependent clause to the main clause. The adjective clause pronouns (also known as relative pronouns) are **who, whom, which, that, and whose.**

   形容詞子句以代名詞(**who**,**whom**,**which**,**that**,**whose**)引導,此代名詞連接形容詞子句和主要子句。

3. There are two different kinds of adjective clauses: Restrictive and Nonrestrictive adjective clauses.

   形容詞子句有兩種:限定用法(restrictive)的形容詞子句和非限定用法的形容詞子句(nonrestrictive)。

Ⅰ Restrictive adjective clauses 形容詞子句限定用法

ⓐ Adjective clause pronouns (relative pronouns) used as the subject of the clause:

形容詞子句的關係代名詞為形容詞子句中的主詞。

- The professor **who/that** is giving a speech right now is considered one of
  形容詞子句

  the most prestigious experts on science.
- John is living in an apartment **which/that** is located on Da Zhi Street.
  形容詞子句
- I know the woman **who/that** works with my younger sister.
  形容詞子句
- The dentist pulled out my tooth **which/that** was causing the trouble.
  形容詞子句
- I am raising a dog **which/that** used to be a stray dog.
  形容詞子句

Rewrite these sentences, inserting the clause in parentheses after the appropriate noun.

改寫下列句子，並將括號內的形容詞子句接在所修飾的名詞之後。

❶ The rice was very good. (which we had for dinner last night)

❷ The newspaper article was about a dog.(which saved two children in a fire)

❸ The man has three cats and a dog. (who lives in the apartment next to mine)

❹ Some employers won't hire applicants. (who dress too casually)

❺ Employees believe that clothing is a form of free expression. (who oppose dress codes)

❻ I live in a town. (which is situated in a valley)

❼ The waiter was polite. (who served us at the restaurant)

❽ I read a novel. (which was interesting)

❾ I ran into an old friend the other day. (who has lived in the U.S. for twenty years)

❿ The instructor always gives me good advice. (who is going to retire)

練習一　解答

❶ The rice which we had for dinner last night was very good.

❷ The newspaper article was about a dog which saved two children in a fire.

❸ The man who lives in the apartment next to mine has three cats and a dog.

❹ Some employers won't hire applicants who dress too casually.

❺ Employees who oppose dress codes believe that clothing is a form of free expression.

❻ I live in a town which is situated in a valley.

❼ The waiter who served us at the restaurant was polite.

❽ I read a novel which was interesting.

❾ I ran into an old friend who has lived in the U.S. for twenty years the other day.

❿ The instructor who is going to retire always gives me good advice.

ⓑ Adjective clause pronouns (relative pronouns) used as the object of the clause:

形容詞子句的關係代名詞為形容詞子句中的受詞，在口說英語中，通常被刪除。

🅒 Janet married a man **that/who/whom/X** she met on a bus.
　　　　　　　　　形容詞子句（met的受詞）
🅒 The woman **that/who/whom/X** Janet was out shopping with last Tuesday
　　　　　　　形容詞子句（'that/who/whom/x'是'with'的受詞）
was her sister-in-law.
🅒 I've been thinking about the questions **that/which/X** you asked me last
　　　　　　　　　　　　　　　　（asked的受詞）形容詞子句
week.
🅒 The picture **that/which/X** I put in Helen's room needs cleaning.
　　　　　　　形容詞子句（put的受詞）

ⓒ Other adjective clause pronouns (relative pronoun): whose, when, where:

🅒 The student **whose composition** I read last night writes well.
　　　　　　　形容詞子句(whose之後要加一個名詞)
🅒 The woman **whose purse** was stolen called the police.
　　　　　　　形容詞子句(whose之後要加一個名詞)
🅒 December is the month **when** the weather is usually the coldest.
　　　　　　　　　　　形容詞子句
🅒 The city **where** they spent their vacation was fabulous.
　　　　　　　形容詞子句

Exercise ❷ 練習二

Give some description about people's careers.

請描述這些人的職業。

❶ A teacher is a person _____

❷ A computer programmer is a person _____

❸ An architect is a person _____

❹ A fashion designer is a person _____

❺ A photographer is a person _____

❻ A journalist is a person _____

❼ An actor is a person _____

❽ A chef is a person _____

❾ A pilot is a person _____

❿ A musician is a person _____

Answers will vary.

For example:

❶ A teacher is a person who has enthusiasm in teaching.

❷ A computer programmer is a person who has received a lot of training in computer techniques.

❸ An architect is a person whose job is to design buildings.

❹ A fashion designer is a person whose job is to make patterns for clothes.

❺ A photographer is a person who takes photographs, especially as a professional or as an artist.

❻ A journalist is a person who writes news reports for newspapers, magazines, television, or radio.

❼ An actor is a person who performs in a play, film, or television program.

❽ A chef is a person who is good at cooking.

❾ A pilot is a person who flies an airplane.

❿ A musician is a person who plays a musical instrument very well.

Exercise 3 練習三

Definitions of holidays: Give definition for each of the following holidays using a restrictive adjective clause.

描述節日：請用限定的形容詞子句定義下列節日。

❶ The Moon Festival is a Chinese holiday…

(that takes place on the fifteenth day of the eighth month on the lunar calendar)

❷ The Dragon Boat Festival is a Chinese holiday…

(that takes place on the fifth day of the fifth month on the lunar calendar)

❸ The Chinese Lunar New Year is a Chinese holiday…

(that takes place on the first day of the first month on the lunar calendar)

❹ Christmas is an international holiday…

(that takes place on the twenty-fifth in December)

❺ Halloween is a celebration…

(that takes place in October)

❶ The Moon Festival is a Chinese holiday that takes place on the fifteenth day of the eighth month on the lunar calendar.

❷ The Dragon Boat Festival is a Chinese holiday that takes place on the fifth day of the fifth month on the lunar calendar.

❸ The Chinese Lunar New Year is a Chinese holiday that takes place on the first day of the first month on the lunar calendar.

❹ Christmas is an international holiday that takes place on the twenty-fifth in December.

❺ Halloween is a celebration that takes place in October.

Exercise
4
練習四

Use relative clauses to complete the sentences.
使用關係子句完成句子。

❶ A good housewife is someone…

❷ A good husband is someone…

❸ A good lover is someone…

❹ A good neighbor is someone…

❺ A good friend is someone…

練習四 解答

Answers will vary.

For example:

❶ A good housewife is someone who would cook and keep the house clean.

❷ A good husband is someone who is responsible for the whole family.

❸ A good lover is someone who is considerate and kind.

❹ A good neighbor is someone who will give you some help.

❺ A good friend is someone who cares you.

II Nonrestrictive adjective clauses　形容詞子句非限定用法（表現唯一、同位語）

注意：使用形容詞子句非限定用法時，記得形容詞子句的前後必須標上逗號。並且that形容詞子句不可用非限定用法。

ⓐ Adjective clause pronouns (relative pronouns) used as the subject of the clause.

形容詞子句的關係代名詞為形容詞子句中的主詞。

- Susan Newman, **who** works at AT&T, is wearing a beautiful dress today.
  形容詞子句非限定用法
- Professor Zhang, **who** teaches Calculus 101, is the chairman of this
  形容詞子句非限定用法
  department.
- Hawaii, **which** consists of eight principal islands, is a fabulous vacation spot.
  形容詞子句非限定用法

ⓑ Adjective clause pronouns (relative pronouns) used as the object of the clause:

形容詞子句的關係代名詞為形容詞子句中的受詞。

- Professor Lee, **whom/who/X** I met yesterday, teaches American Culture.
  形容詞子句非限定用法
- Taipei 101, **which** some people refer to the tallest building in Taiwan, is
  形容詞子句非限定用法
  located in Xin-Yi District in Taipei.

ⓒ Other adjective clause pronouns (relative pronouns):

其他關係代名詞

- We enjoyed Mexico City, **where** we spent our vacation.
  形容詞子句非限定用法
- Mr. David Smith, **whose** son won the first prize in the contest, is the CEO in
  形容詞子句非限定用法
  ABC company.

III Reducing adjective clauses to adjective phrases
形容詞子句改為修飾片語

Only adjective clauses that have a subject pronoun (who, which, or that) could be reduced to modifying adjective phrases.

只有關係代名詞為形容詞子句中的主詞（who，which，或that）的形容詞子句可改為形容詞修飾片語。

① Omit the adjective clause pronoun and verb **be**.

刪除形容詞子句中的關係代名詞和**be**動詞。

② Omit the adjective clause pronoun and, if there is no verb **be**, change the verb to **-ing** form.

若形容詞子句中沒有**be**動詞的話，將關係代名詞刪除後，把一般動詞改為**-ing**的形式。

③ Nonrestrictive adjective clauses can also be changed to adjective phrases.

非限定用法的形容詞子句也可以改為修飾片語，步驟一樣。

- The man <u>who is talking to John</u> is my brother Gary.
        形容詞子句
  ➡ The man <u>talking to John</u> is my brother Gary.
        形容詞修飾片語

- Ms. Sara Johnson is the person <u>who is in charge of the meeting this afternoon</u>.
                    形容詞子句
  ➡ Ms. Sara Johnson is the person <u>in charge of the meeting this afternoon</u>.
                    形容詞修飾片語

- My neighbor <u>who lives next door</u> went on a business trip this morning.
        形容詞子句
  ➡ My neighbor <u>living next door</u> went on a business trip this morning.
        形容詞修飾片語

- English has an alphabet <u>that/which consists of twenty-six letters</u>.
                形容詞子句
  ➡ English has an alphabet <u>consisting of twenty-six letters</u>.
                形容詞修飾片語

● Dr. Sun Yet-Sun, <u>who was the first president of the Republic of China</u>, was
形容詞子句

born in the province of Guang Dueng.

➡ Dr. Sun Yet-Sun, the first president of <u>the Republic of China</u>, was born in the
形容詞修飾片語

province of Guang Dueng.

● Jeremy Lin, <u>who is known as Linsanity</u>, visited Taiwan and held a press
形容詞子句非限定用法

conference in Taipei in August 2012.

➡ Jeremy Lin, <u>known as Linsanity</u>, visited Taiwan and held a press conference
形容詞修飾片語

in Taipei in August 2012.

Exercise 5 練習五

Identify and underline the relative clause in each sentence below.
在下列的句子中,辨認出關係子句並加上底線。

❶ The earrings Jim gave Sue for Christmas must have cost a lot of money.

❷ The phone call I got this morning was from my mother.

❸ The sofa they bought two years ago is falling to pieces already.

❹ The song my sister could not remember the name of was *Unchained Melody*.

❺ David was talking to Dr. Thomson, his academic adviser.

❻ The rent of the apartment Jim lives is high.

❼ A man I met by chance on a business trip to Paris was interesting.

❽ Dr. Peter Davis, the chairman of the committee, is visiting Mexico City next month.

❾ I live in a town situated in a valley.

❿ My younger brother Jimmy, 25, is going to take a business trip to Holland next Monday.

⓫ I am really into the movie I saw last night.

⓬ *Romeo and Juliet* is written by William Shakespeare, a British poet and playwright.

⓭ *Hamlet*, one of the four great tragedies of William Shakespeare's, is my favorite.

⓮ The survey conducted by this university suggested that young children spend at least thirty hours playing computer games.

⓯ David is looking for a job compatible with his style.

❶ The earrings <u>Jim gave Sue for Christmas</u> must have cost a lot of money.

❷ The phone call <u>I got this morning</u> was from my mother.

❸ The sofa <u>they bought two years ago</u> is falling to pieces already.

❹ The song <u>my sister could not remember the name of</u> was Unchained Melody.

❺ David was talking to Dr. Thomson, <u>his academic adviser</u>.

❻ The rent of the apartment <u>Jim lives</u> is high.

❼ A man <u>I met by chance on a business trip to Paris</u> was interesting.

❽ Dr. Peter Davis, <u>the chairman of the committee</u>, is visiting Mexico City next month.

❾ I live in a town <u>situated in a valley</u>.

❿ My younger brother Jimmy, <u>25</u>, is going to take a business trip to Holland next Monday.

⓫ I am really into the movie <u>I saw last night</u>.

⓬ Romeo and Juliet is written by William Shakespeare, <u>a British poet and playwright</u>.

⓭ Hamlet, <u>one of the four great tragedies of William Shakespeare's</u>, is my favorite.

⓮ The survey <u>conducted by this university</u> suggested that young children spend at least thirty hours playing computer games.

⓯ David is looking for a job <u>compatible with his style</u>.

Translation: Translate the following sentences using adjective clauses.
翻譯：使用形容詞子句翻譯下列句子。

❶ 你昨天要我寫的信寫好了。

❷ Ben錯過了往高雄的直達火車。

❸ 我就讀於座落在台北市大直街的實踐大學。

❹ 21歲以下的人不能買酒。

❺ 你要仔細閱讀藥罐上的用藥指示。

❻ 身高110公分以下的孩童可以免費入場看電影。

❼ 王先生就是那位太太是英文老師的人。

❽ 有人拿走你遺留在視聽教室的手機。

❾ 這位就是我向你提過的王太太。

❿ 全台灣最高的大樓台北101大樓已經成為台灣新的觀光景點。

解答

❶ 你昨天要我寫的信寫好了。

I have already finished the letter which you asked me to write yesterday.

❷ Ben錯過了往高雄的直達火車。

en missed the non-stop train heading for Kaohsiung.

❸ 我就讀於座落在台北市大直街的實踐大學。

I am attending Shih Chien University, (which is) located on Da Zhi Street, Taipei.

❹ 21歲以下的人不能買酒。

Anyone (who is) under 21 is prohibited from buying alcohol.

❺ 你要仔細閱讀藥罐上的用藥指示。

You have to read the dosage instructions (which are) on the bottle carefully.

❻ 身高110公分以下的孩童可以免費入場看電影。

Children (who are) under 110 centimeters could have free admission to the movies.

❼ 王先生就是那位太太是英文老師的人。

Mr. Wang is the man whose wife is an English teacher.

❽ 有人拿走你遺留在視聽教室的手機。

Someone took your cell phone which was left in the lab.

❾ 這位就是我向你提過的王太太。

This is Mrs. Wang whom/who I mentioned to you the other day.

❿ 全台灣最高的大樓台北101大樓已經成為台灣新的觀光景點。

Taipei 101, the highest building in Taiwan, has become a new tourist spot.

IV Overview of the Restrictive and Nonrestrictive Adjective Clauses　形容詞子句限定和非限定用法複習

ⓐ The adjective clauses are divided into restrictive and nonrestrictive relative clauses.

Adjective Clauses (Relative Clauses)		
Relative clauses	1.Have a subject and verb. They are dependent clauses. They must be attached to a main clause. 2.They must follow the noun they refer to.	
	Restrictive (Identifying) adjective clauses 限定用法	**Nonrestrictive (Non-identifying) adjective clauses** 非限定用法
Meaning	Distinguish one noun from another. Give definition.	Give extra information about a noun and are separated from that noun by **commas**.
Examples from the above passage	1.The man **who** is talking to John is my brother Gary. 2.The city **where** they spent their vacation was fabulous.	1.Taipei 101, **which** some people refer to the tallest building in Taiwan, is located in Xin-Yi District in Taipei. 2.Professor Zhang, **who** teaches Calculus 101, is the chairman of this department.
Subject relative pronouns	1.When *who, which,* or *that* is the subject of a relative clause. 2.A subject relative pronoun is followed by a verb. The verb agrees with the noun that the subject relative pronoun refers to. *Example:* John is living in an apartment **which/that** is located on Da Zhi Street. 3.The relative pronoun **'that'** can not be used in nonrestrictive relative clauses.	

	Restrictive clauses	Nonrestrictive clauses
Subject relative pronouns (for **people**)	1.that, who *Example:* I know the woman *who/that works at AT&T*. The professor *who/that teaches Chemistry 101* is an excellent lecturer.	1.who *Example:* Susan Newman, *who works at AT&T*, is wearing a beautiful dress today. Professor Wilson, *who teaches Chemistry 101*, is an excellent lecturer.
Subject relative pronouns (for **things, animals, and others**)	2.that, which *Example:* My dentist pulled out the tooth *which/that was causing the trouble*.	2.which *Example:* Bogart starred in the film Casablanca, *which was made in 1942*. Hawaii, *which consists of eight principal islands*, is a fabulous vacation spot.
Object relative pronouns	1.When *who, whom, which,* or *that* is the object of a relative clause, it is an object relative pronoun. 2.Are followed by a subject + verb (phrase). The verb does not agree with the noun that the clause refers to. 3.Can be omitted from restrictive relative clauses	
Object relative pronouns (for **people**)	3.that, who, whom *Example:* Janet married a man *that / who / whom/X she met on a bus*.	3.who, whom *Example:* Professor Zhang, *whom I met yesterdays*, is the chairman of this department.
Object relative pronoun for modifying **things, animals, building,** and others	4.that, which *Example:* I've been thinking about the questions *that/which you asked me last week*.	4.which *Example:* Taipei 101, *which some people refer to the tallest building in Taiwan*, is located in Xin-Yi District in Taipei.

| Other relative pronouns | 5.whose, when, where
Example:
1.The student ***whose composition I read last night*** writes well.
2.The woman ***whose purse was stolen*** called the police.
3.December is the month ***when the weather is usually the coldest***.
4.The city ***where they spent their vacation*** was fabulous. | 5.whose, when, where
Example:
1.We enjoyed Mexico City, where we spent our vacation.
2.Mr. David Smith, ***whose son won the first prize in the contest***, is the CEO in ABC company.
3.Child labor was a social problem in late eighteenth-century England, ***where employment in factories became virtual slavery for children***. |

ⓑ Reducing adjective (restrictive) clauses to adjective phrases:

Only adjective clauses that have a subject pronoun (who, which, or that) could be reduced to modifying adjective phrases.

只有關係代名詞為形容詞子句中的主詞（who，which，或that）的形容詞子句可改為形容詞修飾片語。

	Adjective (Restrictive) Clauses	Adjective Phrases
Omit the relative pronoun and be	The man <u>who is talking to John</u> is from Korea	The man <u>talking to John</u> is from Korea.
Omit the subject pronoun and change the verb to -ing form	English has an alphabet <u>that consists of 26 letters</u>.	English has an alphabet <u>consisting of 26 letters</u>.
Nonrestrictive clauses can also be changed to adjective phrase	Jeremy Lin, <u>who is known as Linsanity</u>, visited Taiwan and held a press conference in Taipei in August 2012.	Jeremy Lin, <u>known as Linsanity</u>, visited Taiwan and held a press conference in Taipei in August 2012.

Notes

Unit 6 Adverb Clauses　副詞子句

Adverb clauses are dependent clauses that begin with a subordinating conjunction and show a relationship to the main clause. An adverb clause can be placed before or after the independent clause; however, DO NOT put a comma before a subordinate clause that follows the main clause.

副詞子句是以附屬連結詞引導的附屬子句，且可表現其與主要子句之關係的子句。一個副詞子句可以放在獨立子句的前面或後面。但是，副詞子句如果是接在主要子句的後面，則兩個子句之間不可以加逗點。

I Words used to introduce adverb clauses　引導副詞子句的字詞

ⓐ referring to time: A present tense, not a future tense, is used in an adverb clause of time.

表示時間關係：在時間副詞子句中，以現在簡單式代替未來式。

when	while	before	after	since	once	until	whenever
every time (that)		by the time (that)		the last time (that)		the first time (that)	
as long as		so long as		as soon as		as	

- **While** I was walking on the street the other day, I ran into an old friend.
- I will tell Larry the truth **by the time** I see him tonight.
- Larry has made a lot of friends **since** he came to Taiwan.
- He will call you **as soon** as he gets home.
- We had to stay in the office **until** we finished the project.
- **The next time** I go to the movie, I will invite you.
- **Once** John gets here, tell him to report to Mr. Smith.
- **Whenever** I see Mary, I give her a smile.
- **Every time** I see Mary, I give her a smile.
- **The first time** I went to Taipei, I stayed at my uncle's home.

ⓑ referring to cause and effect　表示因果關係

because	since	as	as long as	so long as	now that

- John didn't come to school **because** he overslept this morning.
- I decided not to go to the concert **since** I was not interested in rock.

- **Now that** Dave has a car, he could drive to work.
- He would treat us to a meal **as long as** he gets a raise.
- **As** May turns eighteen, she could get a driver's license.

ⓒ referring to opposition　表示矛盾對比關係

even though	although	though	while	whereas

- **(Even) though** the weather was cold, Dave went hiking.
- Sue didn't learn English **though** she lived in L.A. for two years.
- Elephants are huge, **while/whereas** mice are tiny.
- **While/Whereas** mice are tiny, elephants are huge.
- **Although** James was tired, he went to work.

ⓓ referring to condition　表示條件關係

unless	only if	even if	in case	whether or not	if

- I will go hiking **unless** it rains.
- **Only if** it rains, the picnic will be canceled.
- **In case** you need to get in touch with me, I will give you my phone number
- **Whether or not** it is cold, James is going to go fishing tomorrow.
- **If** I don't have enough money to take my trip this summer, I will postpone my trip to next summer.

II Reducing adverb clauses to modifying phrases 副詞子句改為修飾片語

Adverb clauses beginning with *before*, *after*, *since*, and *while* can be changed to modifying phrases.

以*before*，*after*，*since*，和 *while* 引導的副詞子句，可以改為修飾片語。

① Be sure that the subjects in the dependent and the main clauses are identical. Omit the subject in the dependent clause and the *be* form of the verb.

確定副詞附屬子句和主要子句的主詞是相同的，才可以改為修飾片語。

刪除副詞附屬子句的主詞和副詞附屬子句中的be動詞。

② If there is no *be* form of a verb, omit the subject and change the verb to **-ing**.

如果副詞附屬子句中的動詞不含be動詞，則刪除副詞附屬子句中的主詞，再將動詞改為**-ing**。

③ If the proper noun（專有名詞）is used in the dependent clause, delete it and change the pronoun（代名詞）in the main clause into the original proper noun（專有名詞）.

如果副詞附屬子句中的主詞為專有名詞，刪除後再將主要子句中的代名詞改為原來的專有名詞。

> ℮ **While I was walking home**, I ran into an old friend.
> ➡ **While walking home**, I ran into an old friend.
> ℮ **After I finished my homework**, I went to bed.
> ➡ **After finishing my homework**, I went to bed.
> ℮ **After I had finished my homework**, I went to bed.
> ➡ **After having finished my homework**, I went to bed.
> ℮ **Before Jim went to work**, he had a cup of coffee.
> ➡ **Before going to work**, **Jim** had a cup of coffee.
> ℮ **Since Mary came to work at this company last year**, she has made a lot of friends.
> ➡ **Since coming to work at this company last year**, **Mary** has made a lot of friends.

I. Complete the following sentences.

❶ As soon as Martina saw the fire, she _____ (telephone) the fire department.

❷ Tonight I will go to bed after I _____ (finish) my homework.

❸ When my parents _____ (arrive) for a visit tomorrow, they will see our new baby for the first time.

❹ Before Jennifer won the lottery, she _____ (not, enter) any kind of contest.

❺ I borrowed four books on gardening the last time I _____ (go) to the library.

❻ It seems that whenever I travel abroad I _____ (forget) to take something I need.

❼ I'll return Bob's pen to him the next time I _____ (see) him.

❽ Before I started the car, all of the passengers _____ (buckle) their seat belts.

❾ While we _____ (drive) down the gravel road, a small stone struck the windshield.

❿ Ever since Mary arrived, she _____ (sit) quietly in the corner. Is something wrong?

⓫ When I _____ (see) the doctor this afternoon, I will ask him to look at my throat.

⓬ By the time he comes, we _____ (already, leave).

⓭ I _____ (go) to an opera the first time I went to New York.

⓮ The next time I _____ (go) to Hawaii, I'm going to visit Mauna Loa, the world's largest volcano.

⓯ The farmer acted too late. He locked the barn door after his horse _____ (steal).

⑯ A hurricane's force begins to diminish as soon as it _____ (strike) land.

⑰ When I reached my 21st birthday, I _____ (not, feel) any older.

⑱ I _____ (be) late to work three times since my watch broke.

⑲ Before I _____ (leave) for work, I had a cup of tea.

⑳ I _____ (hear) a gunshot while I was waiting for my bus.

II. Reduction of adverb clauses to modifying phrases.

❶ Since Bob opened his new business, he has been working 16 hours a day.

_____

❷ After Nancy had been jogging for twenty minutes, she began to feel tired.

_____

❸ While Tom was washing his new car, he discovered a small dent in the rear fender.

_____

❹ Before I started the car, all of the passengers had buckled their seat belts.

_____

❺ After the police stopped the fight, they arrested two men and a woman.

_____

練習一 解答

I. Complete the following sentences.

❶ As soon as Martina saw the fire, she <u>telephoned</u> (telephone) the fire department.

❷ Tonight I will go to bed after I <u>finish</u> (finish) my homework.

❸ When my parents <u>arrive</u> (arrive) for a visit tomorrow, they will see our new baby for the first time.

❹ Before Jennifer won the lottery, she <u>didn't enter/ hadn't entered</u> (not, enter) any kind of contest.

❺ I borrowed four books on gardening the last time I <u>went</u> (go) to the library.

❻ It seems that whenever I travel abroad I <u>forget</u> (forget) to take something I need.

❼ I'll return Bob's pen to him the next time I <u>see</u> (see) him.

❽ Before I started the car, all of the passengers <u>had buckled / buckled</u> (buckle) their seat belts.

❾ While we <u>were driving</u> (drive) down the gravel road, a small stone struck the windshield.

❿ Ever since Mary arrived, she <u>has been sitting</u> (sit) quietly in the corner. Is something wrong?

⓫ When I <u>see</u> (see) the doctor this afternoon, I will ask him to look at my throat.

⓬ By the time he comes, we <u>will already have left</u> (already, leave).

⓭ I <u>went</u> (go) to an opera the first time I went to New York.

⓮ The next time I <u>go</u> (go) to Hawaii, I'm going to visit Mauna Loa, the world's largest volcano.

⓯ The farmer acted too late. He locked the barn door after his horse <u>had been stolen/ was stolen</u> (steal).

⓰ A hurricane's force begins to diminish as soon as it <u>strikes</u> (strike) land.

⓱ When I reached my 21st birthday, I <u>didn't feel</u> (not, feel) any older.

⓲ I <u>have been</u> (be) late to work three times since my watch broke.

⓳ Before I <u>left</u> (leave) for work, I had a cup of tea.

⓴ I <u>heard</u> (hear) a gunshot while I was waiting for my bus.

II. Reduction of adverb clauses to modifying phrases.

❶ Since Bob opened his new business, he has been working 16 hours a day.
<u>Since opening his new business, Bob has been working 16 hours a day.</u>

❷ After Nancy had been jogging for twenty minutes, she began to feel tired.
<u>After having been jogging for twenty minutes, Nancy began to feel tired.</u>

❸ While Tom was washing his new car, he discovered a small dent in the rear fender.
<u>While washing his new car, Tom discovered a small dent in the rear fender.</u>

❹ Before I started the car, all of the passengers had buckled their seat belts.
<u>No change.</u>

❺ After the police stopped the fight, they arrested two men and a woman.
<u>After stopping the fight, the police arrested two men and a woman.</u>

III Overview of the Adverb Clauses 副詞子句複習

ⓐ A list of words and phrases used to introduce adverb clauses:

導入副詞子句的字和片語

time	cause and effect	opposition	condition
when	because	even though	unless
while	since	although	only if
before	as	though	even if
after	as long as	while	in case
since	so long as	whereas	whether or not
once	now that		if
until			
whenever			
every time (that)			
by the time (that)			
the last time (that)			
the first time (that)			
as long as			
so long as			
as soon as			
as			

ⓑ Reducing adverb clauses to modifying phrases

副詞子句改為修飾片語

Adverb clauses beginning with **_before_**, **_after_**, **_since_**, and **_while_** can be changed to modifying phrases.

以**_before_**，**_after_**，**_since_**，和 **_while_** 引導的附屬子句，可以改為修飾片語。

time	adverb clauses	condition
Be sure that the subjects in the dependent and the main clauses are identical. Omit the subject in the dependent clause and the be form of the verb.	1.While **I was** walking home, I ran into an old friend. 主詞是相同的，可以改為修飾片語。	1.While walking home, I ran into an old friend.

確定附屬子句和主要子句的主詞是相同的，才可以改為修飾片語。刪除附屬子句的主詞和附屬子句中的be動詞。	2.<u>While May was walking home</u>, I ran into an old friend. 主詞不是相同的，不可以改為修飾片語。	2.主詞不是相同的，不可以改為修飾片語。
If there is no *be* form of a verb, omit the subject and change the verb to -ing. 如果附屬子句中的動詞不含be動詞，則刪除附屬子句中的主詞，再將動詞改為-ing。	3.<u>After **I finished** my homework</u>, I went to bed.	3.<u>After finishing my homework</u>, I went to bed.
If the proper noun（專有名詞）is used in the dependent clause, delete it and change the pronoun（代名詞）in the main clause into the original proper noun（專有名詞）. 如果附屬子句中的主詞為專有名詞，刪除後再將主要子句中的代名詞改為原來的專有名詞。	4.Before **Jim went** to work, he had a cup of coffee. 5.Since **Mary came** to work at this company last year, she has made a lot of friends.	4.Before going to work, **Jim** had a cup of coffee. 5.Since coming to work at this company last year, **Mary** has made a lot of friends.

Notes

Unit 7 Conditionals 假設語態

I Present Conditionals (First Conditionals) =Present Real Conditionals 一般假設

A.Sentence Pattern 真實假設

If / When + S + V(simple present)（現在簡單式）, S + V(simple present)（現在簡單式）...

B.Use: The Present Real Conditional is used to talk about what you normally do *in real-life situations*.

- If I **go** to a friend's house for dinner, I usually **take** a bottle of wine or some flowers.
- When I **have** a day off from work, I often **go** to the beach.
- If the weather **is** nice, she walks to **work**.
- Jerry **helps** me with my homework when he **has** time.
- I **read** if there **is** nothing on TV.
- A: What **do you do** when it **rains**?
  B: I **stay** at home.
- A: Where **do you stay** if you **go** to Sydney?
  B: I **stay** with my friends near the harbor.

II Present Unreal Conditionals (Second Conditionals) 與現在事實相反假設

A.Sentence Pattern

If + S + V(simple past)（過去簡單式）, S + would + verb（原形）...

B.Use: The Present Unreal Conditional is used to talk about what you would generally do in imaginary situations.

- If I **owned** a car, I **would drive** to work. (In fact, I don't own a car.)
- She **would travel** around the world if she **had** more money. (In fact, she doesn't have much money.)
- If they **worked** harder, they **would earn** more money.

A: What **would** you **do** if you **won** the lottery?

B: I **would buy** a house.

A: Where **would** you **live** if you **moved** to the U.S.?

B: I **would live** in Seattle.

Exercise 1 練習一

Storytelling Relay.
故事接力。

Tell your classmates what you would do if you had ten million dollars. For example, you may say "If I had ten million dollars, I would buy a house with a big garden." Now, try your own.

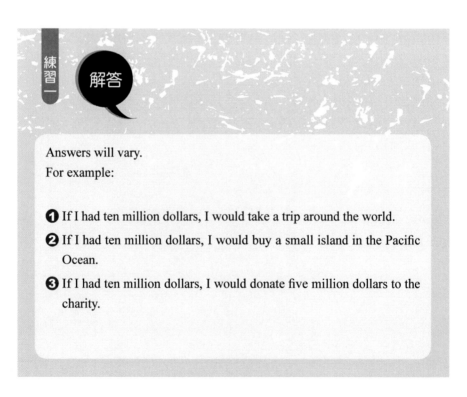

練習一 解答

Answers will vary.
For example:

❶ If I had ten million dollars, I would take a trip around the world.
❷ If I had ten million dollars, I would buy a small island in the Pacific Ocean.
❸ If I had ten million dollars, I would donate five million dollars to the charity.

There are a variety of superstitions and beliefs around the world. They could be true for some people and far-fetched for others. Rewrite the following sentences in your own words. You may use either the first or the second conditionals.

在全球各地流傳著許多不同的迷信和信仰。對某些人來說是確信不疑，但對其他人來說有可能是不可信的。請將下列的句子改寫為假設句。

❶ Throwing salt over your left shoulder brings good luck.

❷ A black cat that walks in front of you brings bad luck.

❸ Thirteen is an unlucky number.

❹ Garlic keeps away vampires or bad luck.

❺ Sleeping in moonlight brings danger.

❻ Breaking a mirror will bring 7 year's bad luck.

❼ To have good luck, you should carry a rabbit's foot.

❽ Some people say the number 13 is unlucky.

❾ If you get sick, you should eat chicken soup.

❿ In Mexico, when scorpions come down from the mountain, the mountain god is angry and soon it will rain.

(Scorpions can feel the wind before people.)

⓫ An old British superstition says, "Never lend milk to anyone. The person might be a witch who will put a magic spell on your cow."

(It means: Don't lend anything to anyone.)

⓬ Many years ago in Brazil, land owners told fruit pickers not to eat mangoes. If they did, they would get sick.

(They said this so the fruit pickers wouldn't eat the fruit they picked.)

⓭ If Japanese children don't cover their stomachs during a storm, the thunder god will steal their belly-buttons.

(During a storm, the temperature goes down. They cover themselves to keep warm.)

⓮ In the United States of America, it is bad luck to say "Good luck!" to an actor. Instead, people say "Break a leg!"

⓯ In Japan, before a match, sumo wrestlers throw salt around the ring to purify it.

練習二 解答

Answers will vary.

For example:

❶ If you throw salt over your left shoulder, it brings good luck to you.

❷ If a black cat walks in front of you, it brings bad luck to you.

❸ If you get number thirteen, it brings you bad luck.

III Past Unreal Conditional　與過去事實相反假設

A. Sentence Pattern

If + S + <u>V(past perfect)</u>（過去完成式）, S + <u>would have + p.p.</u>（現在完成式）...

B. Use: The Past Unreal Conditional is used to talk about imaginary situations in the past. You can describe what *you would have done differently* or how **something could have happened differently** if circumstances had been different.

- If I **had owned** a car, I **would have driven** to work. In fact, I didn't own one; I took the bus to work.
- She **would have traveled** around the world if she **had had** more money. In fact, she didn't have much money; she never traveled.
- I **would have read** more as a child if I **hadn't watched** so much TV. Unfortunately, I did watch a lot of TV, so I never read for entertainment.
- Mary **would have gotten** the job and **moved** to Japan if she **had studied** Japanese in school instead of French.
- If Jack **had worked** harder, he **would have earned** more money. Unfortunately, he was lazy and he didn't earn much.
- A: What **would** you **have done** if you **had won** the lottery last week?

  B: I **would have bought** a house.
- A: What city **would** you **have chosen** if you **had decided** to move to the United States of America?

  B: I **would have chosen** Seattle.

IV Future Unreal Conditionals　與未來事實相反假設

A. Sentence Pattern 1（未來發生機率最高）

1. If + S + <u>V(simple present)</u>（現在簡單式）, S + <u>will/can/may + verb</u>（原形）...
2. If + S + <u>V(simple present)</u>（現在簡單式）, 命令句

B. Sentence Pattern 2（未來發生機率中等值）萬一

1. If + S + <u>should + V</u>（原形）, S + <u>would/could/should/might + verb</u>（原形）...
2. If + S + <u>should + V</u>（原形）, 命令句

C.Sentence Pattern 3（未來發生機率最低）

If + S + <u>were to</u> + V（原形）, S + <u>would/could/should/might</u> + verb （原形）...

- If I have enough money, I will buy a car.
- If I should have enough money, I would buy a car.
- If I were to have enough money, I would buy a car.
- If James calls, tell him I will be back around five.
- If James should call, tell him I will be back around five.
- If James were to call, I would be in my office.

Ⅴ Mixed Conditionals 混合型假設語態

A.過去假設 + 現在結果（如果過去……，現在就……）

If + S + <u>V(past perfect)</u>（過去完成式）, S + <u>would</u> + verb（原形）...

- If I **had won** the lottery, I **would be** rich now.
  (I didn't win the lottery in the past, and I am not rich now.)
  要是之前我有中樂透，我現在就有錢了。
- If I **had taken** French in university, I **would have** more job opportunities.
  (I didn't take French in university, and I don't have many job opportunities.)
  要是我在大學唸書時有學法文，我現在就有更多的就業機會。
- If John **had been born** in the United States, he **would not need** a visa to work in the States.
  (John was not born in the United States, and he needs a visa to work in the States.)
  要是John是在美國出生的話，他現在在美國工作就不需要簽證。
- If I **had had** my breakfast at home this morning, I **would not be** hungry now.
  (I did not have my breakfast at home this morning, and I am hungry now.)
  要是今天上午我在家有吃早餐的話，我現在就不會餓了。

B.過去假設 + 未來結果（如果過去……，未來就……）

If + S+ <u>V(past perfect)</u>（過去完成式）, S + <u>would/could/should/might + verb（原形）</u>…

- If Susan **had signed** up for the yoga class last week, she **would join** us tomorrow.

  (Susan didn't sign up for the yoga class last week, and she is not going to join us tomorrow.)

  上週Susan要是有報名瑜伽課的話，明天她就可以加入我們了。

- If Mike **had gotten** the job, he **would move** to Kaohsiung.

  (Mike didn't get the job, and Mike is not going to move to Kaohsiung.)

  要是Mike得到那份工作的話，那麼Mike就將搬到高雄去了。

- If Dave **hadn't wasted** his year-end bonus gambling in Las Vegas, he **would go** to Hawaii with us next month.

  (Dave wasted his year-end bonus gambling in Las Vegas, and he is not going to Hawaii with us next month.)

  要是Dave之前沒有在Las Vegas輸掉他的年終獎金的話，那麼他下個月就可以和我們一起去Hawaii了。

C.現在假設 + 過去結果（如果現在……，過去就……）

If + S + <u>V(simple past)</u>（現在簡單式）, S + <u>would have + p.p.(現在完成式)</u>…

- If I **were** rich, I **would have bought** that magnificent mansion we saw yesterday.

  (I am not rich currently, and that is why I didn't buy that magnificent mansion we saw yesterday.)

  如果我有錢的話，昨天我一定就會買下我們看到的那一棟宏偉的豪宅。

- If Bob **spoke** Greek, he **would have translated** the letter from your Greek friend for you yesterday.

  (Bob doesn't speak Greek, and that is why he didn't translate the letter from your Greek friend for you yesterday.)

  如果Bob會說希臘文的話，昨天他就會幫你翻譯你那一位希臘朋友的來信。

- If I **didn't have** to work so much this morning, I **would have gone** to the party last night.

  (I have to work a lot this morning, and that is why I didn't go to the party last night.)

  要不是我今天上午有這麼多工作的話，昨晚我一定會去參加派對的。

D.現在假設＋未來結果（如果現在……，未來就……）

 If＋S＋<u>V(simple past)（過去簡單式）</u>, S＋<u>would/could/should/might＋verb（原形）</u>…

- If Jack **didn't have** so much vacation time, he **wouldn't** go with me to Hawaii next week.

  (Jack does have a lot of vacation time, and he will go with me to Hawaii next week.)

  要不是Jack現在有很多的休假的話，他也不可能下星期跟我去Hawaii玩。

- If Jim **were** more creative, the company **would send** him to work on the new advertising campaign.

  (Jim is not creative, and the company will not send him to work on the new advertising campaign.)

  要是Jim有更多的創造力的話，公司將來一定會派他出國去參加商業創意廣告比賽。

- If Maggie **weren't** so nice, she **wouldn't tutor** you in math tomorrow.

  (Maggie is nice, and she is going to tutor you in math tomorrow.)

  要是Maggie不是這麼好的話，她不可能明天願意教你數學。

Exercise 3　練習三

Change the statements to conditional sentences.
請將下列各敘述改為假設語句。

❶ The room is full of flies because you left the door open.

If you _____

❷ Anne got sick because she didn't follow the doctor's orders.

If Anne _____

❸ I don't know anything about plumbing, so I didn't fix the leak in the sink myself.

If I _____

❹ Dave is tired because he didn't go to bed at a reasonable hour last night.

If Dave _____

❺ Jane failed in the test because she didn't prepare for it.

If Jane _____

練習三　解答

❶ The room is full of flies because you left the door open.

If you <u>had closed the door, the room would not be full of flies.</u>

❷ Anne got sick because she didn't follow the doctor's orders.

If Anne <u>had followed the doctor's orders, she would not have got</u> <u>sick.</u>

❸ I don't know anything about plumbing, so I didn't fix the leak in the sink myself.

If I <u>knew anything about plumbing, I would have fixed the leak in</u> <u>the sink myself.</u>

❹ Dave is tired because he didn't go to bed at a reasonable hour last night.

If Dave <u>had gone to bed at a reasonable hour last night, he would not</u> <u>be tired now.</u>

❺ Jane failed in the test because she didn't prepare for it.

If Jane <u>had prepared for the test, she would have passed it.</u>

VI Omitting *If* 刪除 *If*

With ***were, had*** (past perfect), and ***should***, sometimes ***if*** is omitted and the subject and verb are inverted.

刪除 *If* 後，主詞和動詞對調位子，此目的為加強語氣。

- If I were you, I wouldn't do that.
  - ➡ Were I you, I wouldn't do that.
- If I had known that Jim was in Taipei yesterday, I would have informed you.
  - ➡ Had I known that Jim was in Taipei yesterday, I would have informed you.
- If John should call, I would be reached at 555-3245.
  - ➡ Should John call, I would be reached at 555-3245.

In each sentence, underline the if-clause. Circle the verb inside the if-clause and the verb inside the main clause. Add a comma where necessary.
請在下列各句中將If子句畫線,並在If子句中將動詞圈起來,另外將主要子句中的動詞也圈起來,且在需要的地方加上逗點。

❶ If the air temperature drops below freezing the forecast will snow.

❷ If you were locked out call a locksmith to help you.

❸ You should find someone to help you if you are lost in a new big city.

❹ If there is a typhoon approaching toward the city where you are staying at home would be the best policy.

❺ If your boss is making a call in the office you should keep quite.

❻ If you are in a diet you should avoid the fries.

❼ If it rains tomorrow I will take my raincoat.

❽ Andy would have passed the test if he had prepared for it.

❶ If the air temperature drops below freezing, the forecast will snow.

❷ If you were locked out, call a locksmith to help you.

❸ You should find someone to help you if you are lost in a new big city.

❹ If there is a typhoon approaching toward the city where you are, staying at home would be the best policy.

❺ If your boss is making a call in the office, you should keep quite.

❻ If you are in a diet, you should avoid the fries.

❼ If it rains tomorrow, I will take my raincoat.

❽ Andy would have passed the test if he had prepared for it.

Exercise 5 練習五

Fill in the blank with a logical result of the information in the if-clause. Add commas where necessary.

請填入一個合理的結果，以完成句子，並在需要的地方加上逗點。

❶ If you drop an egg, it _____

❷ If you can't drive a car, you _____

❸ If I had time, I _____

❹ If I had received a bad grade in high school, I _____

❺ If the sun were to rise in the west, I _____

練習五 解答

Answers will vary.

For example:

❶ If you drop an egg, it breaks.

❷ If you can't drive a car, you can take a bus.

❸ If I had time, I would go on a vacation.

❹ If I had received a bad grade in high school, I would have cried for at least two days.

❺ If the sun were to rise in the west, I would marry you.

VII Overview of the Conditionals 假設語態複習

Conditionals	Sentence Pattern
I.Present Conditionals (First Conditionals) =Present Real Conditionals真實假設	If / When + S + V(simple present)（現在簡單式）, S + V(simple present)（現在簡單式）...
II.Present Unreal Conditionals (Second Conditionals) 與現在事實相反假設	If + S + V(simple past)（過去簡單式）, S + would + verb（原形）...
III.Past Unreal Conditional 與過去事實相反假設	If + S + V(past perfect)（過去完成式）, S + would have + p.p.（現在完成式）...
IV.Future Unreal Conditionals 與未來事實相反假設	A.Pattern 1（未來發生機率最高） 　1.If + S + V(simple present)（現在簡單式）, 　　S + will/can/may + verb（原形）... 　2. If + S + V(simple present), 命令句 B.Pattern 2（未來發生機率中等值） 　萬一 　1.If + S + should + V（原形）, 　　S + would/could/should/might + verb（原形）... 　2.If + S + should + V（原形）, 命令句 C.Pattern 3（未來發生機率最低） 　If + S + were to + V（原形）, 　S + would/could/should/might + verb（原形）...

V.Mixed Conditionals 混合型假設語態	A.過去假設 ＋ 現在結果（如果過去……，現在就……） If + S + <u>V(past perfect)</u>（過去完成式）， S + <u>would + verb</u>（原形）... B.過去假設 ＋ 未來結果（如果過去……，未來就……） If + S+ <u>V(past perfect)</u>（過去完成式）， S + <u>would/could/should/might + verb</u>（原形）... C.現在假設 ＋ 過去結果（如果現在……，過去就……） If + S + <u>V(simple past)</u>（過去簡單式）， S + <u>would have + p.p.</u>（現在完成式）... D.現在假設 ＋ 未來結果（如果現在……，未來就……） If + S + <u>V(simple past)</u>（過去簡單式）， S + <u>would/could/should/might + verb</u>（原形）...

Part II

Part **II**

基礎段落寫作

Basic Paragraph Writing

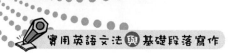

Unit 8 Paragraph Structure 段落結構

When you are writing a paragraph, or an essay, you have to give it a title. A good title tells your readers what they are going to find in the paragraph or essay easily. Remember a good title is usually very short and specific, not too general, and it should not be a sentence. Capitalize first letter of each word in the title, except articles (a, an, the) , conjunctions (and, but, so, for, or, yet, nor) and prepositions (in, on, for, of, off, with, without, under, beneath, ...).

一個好的段落或文章的題目，可以給閱讀者一個概念，讓他們了解他們即將閱讀的內容。切記，一個好的段落或文章的題目，務必要短、範圍要小、並且不可以是個句子。除了冠詞、連接詞、介系詞之外，題目每一個字的第一個字母要大寫。若題目的第一個字是冠詞、連接詞、或介系詞，則不在此限，還是將第一個字母大寫。

There are three parts of a paragraph: a topic sentence, three supporting sentences, and a concluding sentence.

topic sentence（主題句）
supporting sentences（支撐句）
concluding sentence（結論句）

The **topic sentence（主題句）** states the main idea of the paragraph, and usually appears in the first sentence of the paragraph. In the topic sentence, the **topic（主題）** of the paragraph, and a **controlling idea（控制意念）**, which announces the specific area to be discussed in the paragraph, are included.

topic（主題）		*controlling idea*（控制意念）
My roommate Jane	is	considerate.
Convenience foods	are	easy to prepare.
Driving on freeways		requires skill and alertness.
A major problem for many students	is	the high cost of tuition and books.
In my opinion, television commercials for cosmetics		lie to women.
Owning an automobile	is	a necessity for me.

Supporting sentences（支撐句）explain or prove the topic sentence, the controlling idea specifically. Good supporting sentences give information that supports and explains the topic of the paragraph. They answer questions --- who? what? where? when? why? and how? --- and give details. Generally, there are kinds of specific supporting details: examples, statistics, convincing surveys, facts, reasons, and quotations.

Topic sentence: My roommate Jane is considerate.
- Supporting sentences: A.She would turn down the volume when I am studying.
  B.She always cleans the kitchen after she cooks.
  C.She would take phone messages for me when I am out.

A **concluding sentence**（結論句）serves two purposes:

- It tells the readers it's the end of the paragraph.
- It reinforces the important ideas to be remembered by summarizing the main points of the paragraph, or repeating the topic sentence in different phrasing.

Begin the concluding sentence with a phrase that tells the readers that the paragraph is completed.

Transitional words and phrases used at the beginning of concluding sentences:

All in all, ...	In any event, ...	In brief, ...	In sum, ...
Indeed, ...	In other words, ...	In short, ...	Therefore, ...
In conclusion, ...	In summary, ...	To conclude, ...	To sum up, ...
To summarize, ...	It is clear that ...	You can see that ...	Hence, ...
Overall, ...	In the end, ...	These examples show that ...	

- Topic sentence: My roommate Jane is considerate.
- Concluding sentence: Indeed, Jane is a thoughtful person.

Therefore, in the paragraph My Roommate Jane, the outline (段落大綱) would be like the following:

My Roommate Jane

❀ (Topic sentence)	My roommate Jane is considerate.
❀ (Supporting sentences)	A.She would turn down the volume when I am studying.
	B.She always cleans the kitchen after she cooks.
	C.She would take phone messages for me when I am out.
❀ (Concluding sentence)	Indeed, Jane is a thoughtful person.

Read the following paragraph, and answer the questions.
閱讀以下段落，並回答問題。

My Roommate Jane

My roommate Jane is considerate. She would turn down the volume when I am studying. Last Tuesday night, I had a big test on the following day, so I had to study late. She was so nice that she turned down the volume because she didn't want to bother my studying. Besides, Jane always cleans the kitchen after she cooks. Jane likes to cook by herself, and she would always clean the kitchen after cooking. She likes to keep all the cooking utensils in the proper positions. She never leaves it messy. Finally, she would take phone messages for me when I am out. Last night, when I was studying in the library, my mother called. She was so nice that she took the detailed message for me. When I called back, my mother said that Jane was so nice and polite to offer her help. Indeed, Jane is a thoughtful person. I am so lucky to have such a wonderful roommate.

❶ What is the title?

❷ What is the topic sentence? What is the controlling idea?

❸ Circle the transition words and phrases.

❹ What are the supporting sentences?

❺ What is the concluding sentence?

練習一

解答

❶ title: My Roommate Jane

❷ topic sentence: My roommate Jane is considerate.
controlling idea: Considerate.

❸ My roommate Jane is considerate. She would turn down the volume when I am studying. Last Tuesday night, I had a big test on the following day, so I had to study late. She was so nice that she turned down the volume because she didn't want to bother my studying. Besides, Jane always cleans the kitchen after she cooks. Jane likes to cook by herself, and she would always clean the kitchen after cooking. She likes to keep all the cooking utensils in the proper positions. She never leaves it messy. Finally, she would take phone messages for me when I am out. Last night, when I was studying in the library, my mother called. She was so nice that she took the detailed message for me. When I called back, my mother said that Jane was so nice and polite to offer her help. Indeed, Jane is a thoughtful person. I am so lucky to have such a wonderful roommate.

❹ supporting sentences: 1.She would turn down the volume when I am studying.

2.Besides, Jane always cleans the kitchen after she cooks.

3.Finally, she would take phone messages for me when I am out.

❺ concluding sentence: Indeed, Jane is a thoughtful person.

Study the following pairs of sentences and check the one you think would be a good, clear topic sentence for a paragraph.
比較以下各組的主題句，選出一個適當且明確的主題句。

1 a.Exercise is healthful.
b.Bicycling is healthful for three reasons.

2 a.Water skiing is fun.
b.Water skiing requires great skills.

3 a.Smoking is a bad habit.
b.It is difficult to quit smoking for three reasons.

4 a.There are three kinds of bad drivers you see on the streets and highways.
b.There are good drivers and bad drivers on the streets and highways.

5 a.Fast food is extremely popular in the United States, but it is not very good for you.
b.There are a lot of fast food restaurants in the United States.

6 a.The college cafeteria is an inexpensive place to eat.
b.There is a cafeteria in my university.

7 a.I usually pay cash when I shop, but I do not use credit cards.
b.There are three reasons I don't have a credit card.

8 a.In a company, there is a boss and some employees.
b.A good boss has three qualities.

9 a.My mother is a housewife.
b.My mother is a competent career woman.

練習二 解答

❶ b
❷ b
❸ b
❹ a
❺ a
❻ a
❼ b
❽ b
❾ b

Exercise ③ 練習三

Work with a partner. Write a topic sentence on the following topics.
寫出一個適當明確的主題句。

ways to meet people in a new place

ways to waste time

ways to meet my better half

ways that we can conserve energy

kinds of students/teachers/friends/movies I enjoy

advantages of being bilingual/living in a small(big) city

foods that are good for your health

why I _____

Unit 9 Paragraph Outline 段落大綱

A **paragraph outline** (段落大綱) is a helpful guide for writers to use when they write a paragraph. In a paragraph outline, writers can list their ideas in the order in which they are going to write about.

對寫作者來說，段落大綱是一個有用的導引。在段落大綱中，寫作者可將他們的想法，先條列出來，以便在寫作時，能有條理的將他們的意見清楚地表現出來。

A **simple paragraph outline** looks like:
簡略的段落大綱

Title
Topic sentence
A.Main supporting sentence
B.Main supporting sentence
C.Main supporting sentence
Concluding sentence

A more **detailed paragraph outline** might look like this:
詳細的段落大綱

Title
Topic sentence
A.Main supporting sentence
  1.Supporting detail
  2.Supporting detail
  3.Supporting detail
B.Main supporting sentence
  1.Supporting detail
  2.Supporting detail
  3.Supporting detail

C.Main supporting sentence

  1.Supporting detail

  2.Supporting detail

  3.Supporting detail

Concluding sentence

Now read the following paragraph and write an outline.
閱讀以下段落，並寫出詳細的段落大綱。

My Roommate Jane

My roommate Jane is considerate. She would turn down the volume when I am studying. Last Tuesday night, I had a big test on the following day, so I had to study late. She was so nice that she turned down the volume because she didn't want to bother my studying. Besides, Jane always cleans the kitchen after she cooks. Jane likes to cook by herself, and she would always clean the kitchen after cooking. She likes to keep all the cooking utensils in the proper positions. She never leaves it messy. Finally, she would take phone messages for me when I am out. Last night, when I was studying in the library, my mother called. She politely offered her help to take the message for me. I called back after I returned home, and my mother said that Jane was so friendly and polite to help her. Indeed, Jane is a thoughtful person. I am so lucky to have such a wonderful roommate.

Detailed Outline

Title _____

Topic sentence _____

A. Main supporting sentence _____

  1. Supporting detail

_____

2. Supporting detail

_____

3. Supporting detail

_____

B.Main supporting sentence _____

1. Supporting detail

_____

2. Supporting detail

_____

3. Supporting detail

_____

C.Main supporting sentence _____

1. Supporting detail

_____

2. Supporting detail

_____

3. Supporting detail

_____

Concluding sentence _____

My Roommate Jane

My roommate Jane is considerate.

A. She would turn down the volume when I am studying.

　1. Last Tuesday night, I had a big test on the following day, so I had to study late. She was so nice that she turned down the volume.

B. Besides, Jane always cleans the kitchen after she cooks.

　1. Jane likes to cook by herself, and she would always clean the kitchen after cooking.

　2. She likes to keep all the cooking utensils in the proper positions.

C. Finally, she would take phone messages for me when I am out.

　1. Last night, when I was studying in the library, my mother called. She politely offered her help to take the message for me.

Indeed, Jane is a thoughtful person. I am so lucky to have such a wonderful roommate.

Choose one topic and write a detailed outline. Remember your title of the paragraph should be narrow, and the topic sentence should be clear and specific.

選一個主題,並寫出詳細的段落大綱。

❶ It is difficult to quit drinking for some (specify) reasons.

❷ The college cafeteria is an inexpensive place to eat.

❸ A good friend has some (specify) important qualities.

❹ Consider the following (specify) factors when choosing a college.

❺ A good boyfriend/girlfriend has some (specify) important qualities.

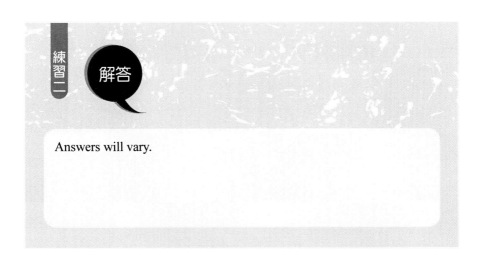

練習二　解答

Answers will vary.

Unit 10 Coherence and Unity 連貫性與單一性

I Coherence 連貫性

In a paragraph, **coherence** is a very important feature because it gives readers a trail to follow. Usually the writers would use transitional words and phrases for the readers to follow along. Transitional words and phrases are essential to maintain the flow and coherence of a paragraph.

在一個段落中連慣性是一個重要的特點，因為它給閱讀者一個可追尋的線索。通常寫作者會利用轉折字或詞來引導閱讀者。這些轉折字或詞是保持段落中的連貫和順暢重要的元素。

Commonly used transitional words and phrases:

1.giving examples:	for example for instance namely
2.emphasizing:	obviously without a doubt for these reasons
3.summarizing:	thus therefore in conclusion in brief all in all indeed in short in the end in other words
4.showing sequence/ importance:	first (second, ...) next first of all at the same time finally after that
5.adding information:	and next in addition moreover furthermore also besides finally
6.showing time:	before after finally after that next
7.comparing or contrasting:	in contrast on the contrary however although even though but on the other hand
8.giving an effect/a result:	therefore consequently as a result thus so
9.giving a cause/reason:	because since for as
10.adding similar ideas:	and also similarly

Exercise 1

 練習一

Add the appropriate transition signals. (in time order or order of importance)
填入適當的表示時間或順序的轉折詞。

Applying for a scholarship is easy as long as you follow these steps.
_____, log on to the university website, and get into the scholarship
office. _____ fill in the application form completely and accurately.
_____ ask two of your instructors to write letters of recommendation
for you. _____, e-mail the application form and turn in letters of
recommendation to the scholarship office before the deadline.

練習一 解答

Applying for a scholarship is easy as long as you follow these steps.
<u>First of all</u>, log on to the university website, and get into the scholarship
office. <u>Second</u>, fill in the application form completely and accurately.
<u>Then</u> ask two of your instructors to write letters of recommendation
for you. <u>Finally</u>, e-mail the application form and turn in letters of
recommendation to the scholarship office before the deadline.

實用英語文法與基礎段落寫作

Exercise 2 練習二

In Exercise 1, underline the topic sentence, circle the supporting sentences. It seems that there is no concluding sentence, so add a concluding sentence.

請在練習一的段落中，畫出主題句、圈出支撐句，並加入一句適當的結論句。

Concluding sentence:

Applying for a scholarship is easy as long as you follow these steps. First of all, log on to the university website, and get into the scholarship office. Second, fill in the application form completely and accurately. Then ask two of your instructors to write letters of recommendation for you. Finally, e-mail the application form and turn in letters of recommendation to the scholarship office before the deadline.

Concluding sentence: (Answers will vary.)
For example: You can see that applying for a scholarship is not difficult at all.

II Unity 單一性

Unity in a paragraph means that all the sentences in a paragraph are related to the topic sentence and, of course, the controlling idea. Make sure the supporting sentences relate to the topic sentence. If there is any sentence which is not related to the topic sentence, delete it.

單一性強調的是段落中的所有句子都要和主題句、控制意念、支撐句相關。若有任何不相關的句子，一律刪除。

Find and cross out any sentences that do not belong in the paragraphs below.

請找出並刪除不相關的句子。

My Brother Gary

I have two brothers: Mark, 23, and Gary, 20. Both of them are university students. I admire Gary a lot. He is 20, and he is very smart, smarter than I am. He majors in international business. When he was an elementary student, he won a prize in a painting competition in Japan. He has been interested in painting, and he is still taking painting lessons in his free time. My brother Mark likes to go jogging. Gary likes to swim. He is a good athlete. He was on the swim team when he was in high school. He has won some swimming prizes too. He often encouraged me to join the swim team. I tried really hard, but I didn't win any prize. In university, he has been a straight A's student. He has great performance in every course he takes. He says that his key to success is concentrating on the one he is doing.

練習二 解答

Cross out the following sentences:

Both of them are university students.

He is 20, and he is very smart, smarter than I am. He majors in international business.

My brother Mark likes to go jogging.

He often encouraged me to join the swim team.

I tried really hard, but I didn't win any prize.

Rearrange and rewrite the paragraph My Brother Gary. Underline the topic sentence, double underline the supporting sentences. Finally, write your own concluding sentence.

請將*My Brother Gary*重組並改寫，請將主題句畫單線，支撐句畫雙線，並加入適當的結論句。

Topic: My Brother Gary

Topic sentence: I admire Gary a lot.

Supporting sentences: He has been interested in painting.

He is a good athlete.

He has been a straight A's student.

Concluding sentence: I am very proud of him.

Unit 11 Process Paragraph 過程段落

When writing a process paragraph, divide a process into separate steps. List or explain the steps in time order --- the order of events as they happen over time. While writing a process paragraph, writers have to

- explain a process in time order,
- presents facts and details in chronological order,
- use transitional words or phrases,
- and give in time warnings.

在寫過程段落時，將整個過程分成幾個步驟來敘述。通常會以時間發生的順序來敘述。記得要加入轉折字或詞，使得過程順暢，並且要給及時的警告。

練 習 一

Read the paragraph and answer the questions.
閱讀以下段落，並回答問題。

How to Make Scrambled Eggs

　　It is very easy to make scrambled eggs if you follow the steps. Before you cook, you need some ingredients: eggs, milk, some salt, and cooking oil. Prepare the following utensils as well: a mixing bowl, a pair of chopsticks, a plate, a cooking shovel, and a frying pan. First, break the eggs into the bowl, and add milk and some salt. If you are thirsty, drink some juice or water. Next, beat the mixture with chopsticks until it is well mixed. Then pour about three tablespoons of cooking oil into the frying pan over low heat. Now, pour the egg mixture into the pan, and let it heat through. Remember you have to turn up the heat slightly. While the eggs cook, push them around with the chopsticks or the cooking shovel. Be gentle, or the eggs will break into pieces. In about three minutes, turn the eggs over and cook them for two more minutes. When the scrambled eggs are done, they should be fluffy. Finally, take them out and place them onto the plate. You can see that the perfect scrambled eggs are done easily, and now enjoy your delicious meal. If you have some more time, you may have some more boiled eggs.

❶ What is the topic sentence of the paragraph? What is the controlling idea?
❷ What are the supporting sentences?
❸ Are there any transitional words or phrases? Circle them.
❹ Is this paragraph coherent? If not, give suggestions.
❺ Are there any irrelevant sentences? If yes, delete them.
❻ Does the writer give any warning?
❼ What is the concluding sentence?
❽ Is there anything that should be added?
❾ Write a detailed outline.

練習一 解答

❾ a detailed outline :

How to Make Scrambled Eggs

It is very easy to make scrambled eggs if you follow the steps.

A.First, break the eggs into the bowl, and add milk and some salt.

B.Next, beat the mixture with chopsticks until it is well mixed.

C.Then pour about three tablespoons of cooking oil into the frying pan over low heat.

D.Pour the egg mixture into the pan, and let it heat through.

    1.Remember you have to turn up the heat slightly.

    2.While the eggs cook, push them around with the chopsticks or the cooking shovel.

        (1)Be gentle, or the eggs will break into pieces.

E.In about three minutes, turn the eggs over and cook them for two more minutes.

F.Finally, take them out and place them onto the plate.

You can see that the perfect scrambled eggs are done easily, and now enjoy your delicious meal.

❺ irrelevant sentences:

If you are thirsty, drink some juice or water.

If you have some more time, you may have some more boiled eggs.

Exercise 2 練習二

Read the paragraph and answer the questions.
閱讀以下段落，並回答問題。

Applying to a University Abroad

The process for applying to a university abroad is not complicated, but it is important to follow each step. The first step is to choose some universities that you are interested in attending. Next, visit their web sites and read the course descriptions thoroughly. If you have come up with some questions, e-mail to the department office or to the admission office. After this research, narrow your list to between three and five universities. Then prepare all the required forms and documents, and mail them to the universities on your final list. If the universities require you to take a standardized test, such as the SAT, ACT, or TOEFL, be sure to take the test early. In addition, ask your supervisors or teachers to write letters of recommendation for you if they are required. Furthermore, almost all universities have an application fee. This fee should be sent in the form of a check or money order. Finally, be sure to finish this application before the deadline. Now, you can see that it is easy to apply to a university abroad as long as you follow the steps.

❶ What is the topic sentence of the paragraph? What is the controlling idea?
❷ What are the supporting sentences?
❸ Are there any transitional words or phrases? Circle them.
❹ Is this paragraph coherent? If not, give suggestions.
❺ Are there any irrelevant sentences? If yes, delete them.
❻ Does the writer give any warning?
❼ What is the concluding sentence?
❽ Is there anything that should be added?
❾ Write a detailed outline.

❾ a detailed outline :

Applying to a University Abroad

The process for applying to a university abroad is not complicated, but it is important to follow each step.

A. The first step is to choose some universities that you are interested in attending.

B. Next, visit their web sites and read the course descriptions thoroughly.

    1. If you have come up with some questions, e-mail to the department office or to the admission office.

C. After this research, narrow your list to between three and five universities.

D. Then prepare all the required forms and documents, and mail them to the universities on your final list.

    1. If the universities require you to take a standardized test, such as the SAT, ACT, or TOEFL, be sure to take the test early.

E. In addition, ask your supervisors or teachers to write letters of recommendation for you if they are required.

F. Furthermore, almost all universities have an application fee.

    1. This fee should be sent in the form of a check or money order.

G. Finally, be sure to finish this application before the deadline.

Now, you can see that it is easy to apply to a university abroad as long as you follow the steps.

Exercise 3

練習三

Choose a topic and write a process paragraph.

選擇一個主題，並寫一個過程段落。

How to make a dish

How to take a good photograph

How to transplant a tree

How to make friends in a new place

How to _____

Unit 12 Cause and Effect Paragraph 因果段落

A cause-effect paragraph explains the reasons that a certain action of event occurs or the results, effects, or consequences of an action.

因果文體的段落寫作主要是用來解釋某件事件產生的原因，或某個行為的結果或影響。把握將其產生的原因，或其結果或其影響清楚解釋的原則即可。

Read the paragraph and answer the questions.
閱讀以下段落，並回答問題。

Why I Agree with Capital Punishment

When I consider capital punishment, I have to admit that I do agree with it. Although it is true that some people will not commit a crime because they are afraid of capital punishment, I am sure that this is the best way to handle those people who commit a crime. I have two reasons that I am for capital punishment. The first reason is fairness. In most cases, people who kill some other people should pay for their behavior, especially those people who are trying to get away from their crime and do not confess their misbehavior. In the long run, the society will become a chaos, and there will be no justice. Next, the second reason is for the economical reason. If there is no capital punishment, the government will have to spend a lot of money keeping those criminals in prison. In other words, a great portion of the budget of a nation is spent on them. Other law-abiding people, on the other hand, have to work hard to keep those criminals alive. Consequently, it will destroy the economy of a country. In sum, I do agree with capital punishment because it is a way to be fair for people and keep economy steady for the whole country.

❶ What is the topic sentence of the paragraph?

❷ What is the controlling idea?

❸ What are the supporting sentences?

❹ Are there any transitional words or phrases? Circle them.

❺ Is this paragraph coherent? If not, give suggestions.

❻ Are there any irrelevant sentences? If yes, delete them.

❼ What are the reasons the writer gives?

❽ What is the concluding sentence? Do you have any better suggestion?

❾ Is there anything that should be added?

練習一　解答

❶ topic sentence: I have two reasons that I am for capital punishment.

❷ controlling idea: I am for capital punishment.

❸ supporting sentences: (two reasons)

                 The first reason is fairness.

                 Next, the second reason is for the economical

                 reason.

❽ concluding sentence: In sum, I do agree with capital punishment

                                because it is a way to be fair for people and

                                keep economy steady for the whole country.

Exercise 2 練習二

The following paragraph is a draft of a student's. Read the paragraph (ignore the mistakes and errors) and answer the questions.

以下為一個學生所寫的段落草稿，閱讀此段落並回答問題。

My Favorite Season

There are four seasons in a year. Among these seasons, my favorite season is summer. First, summer is the hottest season in the four seasons. Sunshine in the summer season gives me hope. Summer is a season always with the sunshine. And I love all my summer clothing and all the beautiful colors that go around in this season. However, summer is the season that let people have the energy in the four seasons. The vegetation and fruits are harvested. The flowers are blooming, trees fully leaved, and the days are arm. And my favorite fruits in summer are watermelon and mango. In the summer, it shows me that there is always a new beginning and that gives me hope. Second, it's time for summer vacation. During the summer vacation I can do a lot of things that I usually don't have time to do. I like to go to the mountains with my family for hiking on the trail. I like both sides of the trail are shadowed by trees. Therefore we will feel no heat at all even in the summer. I particularly like to look around for the trees and to breathe the clean air. I think this sport is very good to our health. I can also go to seashore and swimming pool to play with my friends. The sea will be glittering under the sun and I am very touched by such scenery. I like to go to the swimming pool. My body in the swimming pool will appease all the summer heat. Besides, I can eat ice-cream or drink cold drink in summer. Third, my birthday is in the summer. It's my day. The day means I grow up. It's very excited and happy day. And my friends will celebrate to me. I will have a small party with my friends. I can eat a lot of desserts and cakes. And, I can get many birthday presents. The moment I most like is that I can make the wishes. There are the reasons why I like summer. Summer is my favorite season.

❶ What is the topic sentence of the paragraph?

❷ What is the controlling idea?

❸ What are the supporting sentences?

❹ Are there any transitional words or phrases? (indicating order) Circle them.

❺ Is this paragraph coherent? If not, give suggestions.

❻ Are there any irrelevant sentences? If yes, delete them.

❼ What are the causes the writer mentions?

❽ What is the concluding sentence? Do you have any better suggestion?

❾ Is there anything that should be added?

練習二 解答

❶ topic sentence: My favorite season is summer.

❷ controlling idea: reasons why summer is my favorite season

❸ supporting sentences: (three reasons)

First, sunshine in the summer season gives me hope.

Second, there is a summer vacation.

Third, I was born in summer.

❽ concluding sentence: In sum, these are the reasons why I like summer.

The following paragraph is a draft of a student's. Read the paragraph (ignore the mistakes and errors) and answer the questions.
以下為一個學生所寫的段落草稿,閱讀此段落並回答問題。

Two Major Reasons That People Stop Being Friends

The first and in my opinion the most common reason why people stop being friends is jealousy. Jealousy and rivalry ruin friendships and lead to personal mistakes. Life sometimes likes to be cruel for some people and generous for others and that can be devastating when it comes to friendship. When one for example becomes successful at work, or gets high grades at school without working hard and the other one feels like everything in against him even though he is trying to become successful very hard. He starts to feel jealous for the one that gets everything easily. When there is a jealousy between friends it can finish the friendship very quickly. Different point of view is the second thing that can cause friendship breakup. Sometimes when somebody can't agree with their friend in many areas of life, and if it happens very often they just can't get along anymore. They are arguing all the time and sometimes even become enemies. Point of view is the way we look at the world around us, and when somebody doesn't see it the same way, we feel that we have nothing in common with that person, especially if it is our friend. Different point of view can change the friendship and very often it can be easily end, if we won't understand that everyone is different and has a right to see some things differently than we are. Jealousy, change of marital status, and different point of view leads to the friendship breakup. It doesn't have to be like that, but people very often don't want to deal with problems and overcome them, they just cut the cord and move on with new friends. That is why at some point of life people realize that they don't have any friends present in their life. And that is something that we should think about.

❶ What is the topic sentence of the paragraph?

❷ What is the controlling idea?

❸ What are the supporting sentences?

❹ Is this paragraph coherent? If not, give suggestions.

❺ What is the concluding sentence?

❶ topic sentence: There are two major reasons that people stop being friends.

❷ controlling idea: two major reasons

❸ supporting sentences: The first and the most common reason why people stop being friends is jealousy.
Different point of view is the second reason that causes people stop being friends.

❺ concluding sentence: In sum, people stop being friends because of jealousy and different point of view.

Choose a topic and write a cause-effect paragraph.
選擇一個主題，並寫一個因果段落。

the effects of learning to speak a second language fluently

the effects of playing online games

the effects of learning foreign languages

the causes of car accidents

the causes/effects of _____

why students should not cut class

why I lie to my parents

why _____

Notes

Unit 13 Comparison/Contrast Paragraph 比較／對比段落

In a comparison paragraph, two items, subjects, things, or ideas are compared. Usually it would show the similarities and/or differences between the two subjects. While comparing the two subjects, writers may use one of the two methods: **point-by point method** or **block method** .

比較或對比段落是比較或對比兩件事、物、或個體的寫作文體。一般來說，可以兩件事、物、或個體的相同或相異之處來著手。寫作者可選擇**逐項比較**（**point-by-point method**）或**個別比較**（**block method**）的方式來寫。

point-by-point method (逐項比較) vs. **block method** (個別比較)

Similarities/differences	Subject 1	subject 2
A	1	2
B	1	2
C	1	2

In the **point-by-point method (逐項比較)**, similarity/difference A of subject 1 would be described first, then similarity/difference A of subject 2 would be described. After the similarity/difference A is described, similarity/difference B of subject 1 and subject 2 would be described continuously. Finally, similarity/difference C of subject 1 and subject 2 would be described.

On the other hand, in the **block method (個別比較)**, the similarities/differences A, B, and C of subject 1 would be discussed separately first, then the discussion of the similarities/differences A, B, and C of subject 2 would follow. However, sometimes the specific similarities or differences and the degree of similarity or difference would not be clearly compared or contrasted.

No matter which method the writer uses, the order of discussion should not be changed randomly. Otherwise, the readers would be confused because there is no logic order to follow.

Comparison structure words and phrases (比較類似)					
similarly	likewise	also	too	as	just as
just like	the same	alike	similar to	equally	both…and
not only…but also	like	in addition	in addition to		

1. Tokyo is the financial heart of Japan. Similarly/likewise, Taipei is the center of banking and finance in Taiwan.
2. Tokyo is the financial heart of Japan; similarly/likewise, Taipei is the center of banking and finance in Taiwan.
3. Both Tokyo and Taipei are the centers of banking and finance.
4. You can buy designer clothes not only in boutiques but also in department stores.
5. Taipei is crowded and noisy just as Tokyo is.
6. The two cities are both crowded and noisy.
7. Milan is a center of fashion and style. Tokyo is, too.
8. Milan is a center of fashion and style, and Tokyo is, too.

Contrast structure words and phrases (對比)				
on the other hand	in contrast (to)	however	but	yet
although/though	even though	while	whereas	unlike
on the contrary	nevertheless	conversely		

1. John excels at math. In contrast, James is better at language.
2. John excels at math. In contrast to John, James is better at language.
3. John excels at math, but James is better at language.
4. Elephants are huge, while/whereas mice are tiny.
5. Elephants are huge; on the contrary/however/on the other hand, mice are tiny.
6. Elephants are huge; unlike elephants, mice are tiny.
7. Although elephants are huge, mice are tiny.
8. Elephants are huge. On the other hand/However/On the contrary, mice are tiny.

Read the paragraph and answer the questions.
閱讀以下段落，並回答問題。

My Two Sons

I have two sons: James, 22, and Robert, 20. They are good boys, but they are different in some ways. First of all, they have different personalities. James is introverted; however, Robert is extroverted. James has a few good friends and he goes out with them once in a while, but Robert has a lot of good friends and he hangs out with them often. The second difference is interests. James is interested in math and biology, and he is organized and used to keep beetles and insects as his pets; on the contrary, Robert likes literature and drawing. He likes Chinese literature particularly, and he is good at drawing and won some prizes when he was in high school. Finally, they have different future plans. James would like to go for advanced studies in mechanics and be an engineer in the future. Nevertheless, Robert would like to be a writer since he is really into it. Indeed, no matter what they are like or what they are going to be in the future, they ARE my sons.

❶ What is the topic sentence of the paragraph?

❷ What is the controlling idea?

❸ What are the supporting sentences?

❹ What is the concluding sentence?

❺ Which method does the writer use in writing, point-by point method or block method?

❻ Write a detailed outline.

❶ topic sentence: They are good boys, but they are different in some ways.

❷ controlling idea: different

❸ supporting sentences: First of all, they have different personalities.
The second difference is interests.
Finally, they have different future plans.

❹ concluding sentence: Indeed, no matter what they are like or what they are going to be in the future, they ARE my sons.

❺ point-by point method

❻ a detailed outline:

My Two Sons

They are good boys, but they are different in some ways.

A.First of all, they have different personalities.

   1.James is introverted; however, Robert is extroverted.

   2.James has a few good friends and he goes out with them once in a while, but Robert has a lot of good friends and he hangs out with them often.

B.The second difference is interests.

   1.James is interested in math and biology, and he is organized and used to keep beetles and insects as his pets; on the contrary, Robert likes literature and drawing. He likes Chinese literature particularly, and he is good at drawing and won some prizes when he was in high school.

C.Finally, they have different future plans.

   1.James would like to go for advanced studies in mechanics and be an engineer in the future. Nevertheless, Robert would like to be a writer since he is really into it.

Indeed, no matter what they are like or what they are going to be in the future, they ARE my sons.

Work with a partner. Choose a topic, write a detailed outline and a comparison/ contrast paragraph.
選擇一個主題，並寫出詳細的段落大綱和對比段落。

❶ Compare the cuisine of one country with the cuisine of another country.

❷ Compare/contrast two important people that you admire.

❸ Compare/contrast two of your siblings/friends.

❹ Compare/contrast two novels/books/movies.

❺ Compare/contrast two school systems/sports players/electrical appliances.

❻ Compare/contrast two _____

Notes

Unit 14 Classification Paragraph　分類段落

A classification paragraph separates ideas into different categories. Writers give a clear classification rule to classify one object into some categories with no overlap. It would be a good idea to give each separated category a distinct description, and if possible, give a clear but simple title or name of each category. Usually there is more than one way to classify a group of items, and the controlling idea tells the basis of the writers' categorization.

分類段落寫作一定要有一個明確清楚的分類原則。寫作者要有一個能將主題明確分類的原則。以分類原則分類後，給予每一個類別一個描述或名稱，可以讓閱讀者更瞭解寫作者的分類概念。

Read the paragraph and answer the questions.

閱讀以下段落，並回答問題。

Types of Movies I Like Most

There are several types of movies, but I like only three types of them. The first type of movies I like most is romantic movies. In this kind of movies, there is always a beautiful, romantic, and touching story appealing all the movie goers. The most famous examples of this type of film are *Romeo and Juliet* and *Titanic*. In these two movies, the romantic love between two young people touches the hearts of all the audience. The second type of movies I like most is science-fiction. The feature of this type of movies is people's imagination. The story line for the film has been invented. The characters and plots are not real, and the stories often present fantasy-type scenarios. One such example is the *Batman* series for everyone knows that Batman is not a real person. Finally, there is another type of movies I like; that is, the animated movies. In this type of film, all the animation is done with computers, and they use the voices of some really famous actors and actresses. That really makes the movie enjoyable. Perhaps the amazing examples of this type of film are *Shrek* and *Up*. In these movies, the audience would be amused by the plots and the computer techniques. All in all, my favorite types of movies: romantics, science-fictions, and animations, always make my life substantial and colorful.

❶ What is the topic sentence of the paragraph?

❷ What is the controlling idea?

❸ What are the supporting sentences?

❹ What is the concluding sentence?

❺ Write a detailed outline.

練習一 解答

❶ topic sentence: There are several types of movies, but I like only three types of them.

❷ controlling idea: I like only three types of them.

❸ supporting sentences: The first type of movies I like most is romantic movies.
The second type of movies I like most is science-fiction.
Finally, there is another type of movies I like; that is, the animated movies.

❹ concluding sentence: All in all, my favorite types of movies: romantics, science-fictions, and animations, always make my life substantial and colorful.

❺ a detailed outline:

Types of Movies I Like Most

There are several types of movies, but I like only three types of them.

A. The first type of movies I like most is romantic movies.
1. In this kind of movies, there is always a beautiful, romantic, and touching story appealing all the movie goers.
2. The most famous examples of this type of film are *Romeo and Juliet* and *Titanic*.

B. The second type of movies I like most is science-fiction.
1. The feature of this type of movies is people's imagination.
2. The story line for the film has been invented. The characters and plots are not real, and the stories often present fantasy-type scenarios.
3. One such example is the *Batman* series for everyone knows that Batman is not a real person.

C. Finally, there is another type of movies I like; that is, the animated movies.
1. In this type of film, all the animation is done with computers, and they use the voices of some really famous actors and actresses.
2. Perhaps the amazing examples of this type of film are *Shrek* and *Up*.

All in all, my favorite types of movies: romantics, science-fictions, and animations, always make my life substantial and colorful.

Exercise ❷ 練習二

The following paragraph is a draft of a student's. Read the paragraph (ignore the mistakes and errors) and answer the questions.
以下為一個學生所寫的段落草稿，閱讀此段落並回答問題。

Types of students

There are several types of students. However, the types of students are hard to giving the meaning, we can according to the habits of students to classify the types of students. First, there are some students who having a best performance on school. They study hard, and won't be absent in class. Also focus on the teacher until the end of class. Compare to the first one, this type of students are the poor students. They don't like to study, and sometimes absent on class. The last type of students is mix first and second. They are good student, and also having no absent on class. But they like to chat in class. Makes teacher have had a bad impressions. I think no matter which types of the students we are, we have to know our duty is study hard and do our best performance on our school.

❶ What is the topic sentence of the paragraph?

❷ What is the controlling idea?

❸ What are the supporting sentences?

❹ What is the concluding sentence?

❺ Write a detailed outline.

練習二 解答

❶ topic sentence: There are three types of students.

❷ controlling idea: I classify students into three types according to the their school performance.

❸ supporting sentences: First, the first type of students is students who have excellent performance at school.
The second type of students is poor-performed students.
The last type of students is the average students.

❹ concluding sentence: It is clear that no matter which types of students they are, students should be responsible for what they are doing.

Exercise
3
練習三

Choose a topic and write a detailed outline and a classification paragraph.
選擇一個主題，並寫出一個詳細的大綱和分類段落。

❶ types of restaurants/foods/fruits/cars I like

❷ types of shoppers/men/women

❸ types of students/teachers/TV programs/holidays

❹ types of TV commercials/advertisements/families/recreations

❺ types of _____

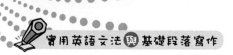

Appendix 1

GUIDE FOR CORRECTING WRITING ERRORS

❶ W. W.: wrong word(s)

❷ W. F.: word form / derivation

❸ W. O.: word order

❹ W+: add word(s)

❺ W-: omit word(s)

❻ V. Tns. / Tns.: verb tense

❼ N - C: noun - countable

❽ N - U: noun - uncountable

❾ Sp.: spelling error

❿ Pun.: punctuation

⓫ Cap.: capitalization

⓬ de-Cap.: de-capitalization

⓭ Art.: articles

⓮ 2 - V: two verbs

⓯ 2 - Aux.: two auxiliary verbs

⓰ 2 - S: two subjects

⓱ S - V Agr.: subject - verb agreement

⓲ Pro. Agr.: pronoun agreement

⓳ Agr.: agreement

⓴ Incomp. Sent./ Frag.: incomplete sentence/fragment

㉑ Run-on (Sent.): run-on sentence

㉒ com-spl.: comma splice

㉓ Reph.: rephrase

㉔ [　]?: meaning not clear

㉕ Transi. +: add some transitional expressions

㉖ Paral.: parallel

㉗ IR: irrelevant

㉘ No - V.: no verb

㉙ No - S.: no subject

㉚ Re.: rewrite

㉛ 0: space

㉜ -----: deletion

㉝ ⌐⌐⌐: reverse

㉞ ⊄: another paragraph

㉟ See me.: See the instructor right after class.

Appendix 2

PEER REVIEW CHECKLIST ------ PARAGRAPH-1

Date: _____

Writer: No. _____   Name: _____

Reviewer: No. _____   Name: _____   Grade: _____

❶ What is the topic of the paragraph? Is it narrowed down enough? Could it be narrowed down further?

_____

❷ What is the topic sentence of the paragraph? (State the topic sentence in your own words if it is implied.)

_____

_____

❸ What is the controlling idea of the paragraph? Is it clear and focused? Do you have any suggestions for improving the controlling idea?

_____

_____

❹ Is the paragraph unified? Do all of the sentences support the controlling idea?

_____

If not, point out sentences that are irrelevant.

_____

_____

_____

❺ Is the paragraph coherent? Are the ideas logically arranged? Does the paragraph flow smoothly?

If not, suggest your ways to improve coherence.

❻ What is the most interesting part of the paragraph?

❼ What has the writer done well?

References 參考書籍

❶ Azar, Betty Schrampfer Understanding and Using English Grammar 2nd edition. New Jersey: Pretice-Hall, Inc., 1989.

❷ Folse, Keith, Solomon, Elena Vestri, & Clabeaux, David Great Writing 3: From Great Paragraphs to Great Essays 2nd Edition. Boston. Heinle, Cengage Learning, 2010.

❸ Folse, Keith, Solomon, Elena Vestri, & Muchmore-Vokoun, April Great Writing 2: Great Paragraphs 3rd Edition. Boston. Heinle, Cengage Learning, 2010.

❹ Hogue, Ann & Oshima, Alice Introduction to Academic Writing 3rd Edition. New York: Person Education, Inc., 2007.

實踐大學數位出版合作系列

語文學習類　PD0014

實用英語文法與基礎段落寫作
Practical English Grammar
and Basic Paragraph Writing

編　　者 / 曾春鳳
統籌策劃 / 葉立誠
文字編輯 / 王雯珊
封面設計 / 陳佩蓉
執行編輯 / 陳彥廷
圖文排版 / 賴英珍

發 行 人 / 宋政坤
法律顧問 / 毛國樑　律師
出版發行 / 秀威資訊科技股份有限公司
　　　　　114台北市內湖區瑞光路76巷65號1樓
　　　　　電話：+886-2-2796-3638　傳真：+886-2-2796-1377
　　　　　http://www.showwe.com.tw
劃撥帳號 / 19563868　戶名：秀威資訊科技股份有限公司
　　　　　讀者服務信箱：service@showwe.com.tw
展售門市 / 國家書店（松江門市）
　　　　　104台北市中山區松江路209號1樓
　　　　　電話：+886-2-2518-0207　傳真：+886-2-2518-0778
網路訂購 / 秀威網路書店：http://www.bodbooks.com.tw
　　　　　國家網路書店：http://www.govbooks.com.tw

2013年3月BOD一版
定價：250元
版權所有　翻印必究
本書如有缺頁、破損或裝訂錯誤，請寄回更換

Copyright©2013 by Showwe Information Co., Ltd.
Printed in Taiwan
All Rights Reserved

國家圖書館出版品預行編目

實用英語文法與基礎段落寫作 / 曾春鳳編著. -- 一版. --
臺北市 : 秀威資訊科技, 2013.03
　　面；　公分
BOD版
ISBN 978-986-326-055-4(平裝)

1. 英語　2. 語法　3. 寫作法

805.16   101027068

讀者回函卡

感謝您購買本書，為提升服務品質，請填妥以下資料，將讀者回函卡直接寄回或傳真本公司，收到您的寶貴意見後，我們會收藏記錄及檢討，謝謝！
如您需要了解本公司最新出版書目、購書優惠或企劃活動，歡迎您上網查詢或下載相關資料：http:// www.showwe.com.tw

您購買的書名：_____

出生日期：_____年_____月_____日

學歷：□高中 (含) 以下　　□大專　　□研究所 (含) 以上

職業：□製造業　□金融業　□資訊業　□軍警　□傳播業　□自由業
　　　□服務業　□公務員　□教職　　□學生　□家管　　□其它_____

購書地點：□網路書店　□實體書店　□書展　□郵購　□贈閱　□其他

您從何得知本書的消息？

　□網路書店　□實體書店　□網路搜尋　□電子報　□書訊　□雜誌
　□傳播媒體　□親友推薦　□網站推薦　□部落格　□其他_____

您對本書的評價：(請填代號　1.非常滿意　2.滿意　3.尚可　4.再改進)

　封面設計____　版面編排____　內容____　文／譯筆____　價格____

讀完書後您覺得：

　□很有收穫　□有收穫　□收穫不多　□沒收穫

對我們的建議：_____

_____

_____

_____

請貼
郵票

11466
台北市內湖區瑞光路 76 巷 65 號 1 樓
秀威資訊科技股份有限公司　　　收
BOD 數位出版事業部

··

（請沿線對折寄回，謝謝！）

姓　　名：＿＿＿＿＿＿＿＿＿　年齡：＿＿＿＿＿　性別：□女　□男

郵遞區號：□□□□□

地　　址：＿＿＿＿＿＿＿＿＿＿＿＿＿＿＿＿＿＿＿＿＿＿＿＿

聯絡電話：(日) ＿＿＿＿＿＿＿＿＿＿＿ (夜) ＿＿＿＿＿＿＿＿＿＿＿

E-mail：＿＿＿＿＿＿＿＿＿＿＿＿＿＿＿＿＿＿＿＿＿＿＿